Fit to Be
TIED

Fairy Tales of a Trailer Park Queen
Book 13

Kimbra Swain

Kimbra Swain
Fit to Be Tied, Fairy Tales of a Trailer Park Queen, Book 13

ASIN: B07RZM79XB

Kimbra Swain / Crimson Sun Press, LLC
kimbraswain@gmail.com

Cover by: Audrey Logsdon
Formatting by: Crimson Sun Graphics
Editing by Carol Tietsworth: https://www.facebook.com/Editing-by-Carol-Tietsworth-328303247526664/

PROLOGUE

I LOOKED UP FROM THE BOOK WITH TEARS IN MY EYES.

"Damn, Levi," I muttered.

"We did what we did for you," he said.

"I'm so sorry." I'd just finished reading his story of what happened in the Otherworld. He'd been tortured along with Dylan. He'd been made to do things to keep Winnie safe. And through it all, he remained a pure untainted heart.

"Nothing was more important than protecting Winnie and you. Dylan and I agreed on at least that one point. I admit that it was brutal, and I don't care to revisit those memories. Once I wrote them down in that book, I decided to absolve myself of what happened. Most of it was beyond my control. The rest, I chose to do in order to save those that I loved," he said.

I placed my hand on his face, looking through the glamour that he used to hide his scar. I'd wondered why he had chosen to hide it along with the scars on his body. After reading the book, I knew that he'd come to terms with the evil that happened and the things he'd done to survive. For all my strength, I couldn't have done what he did. Tracing the scar from his forehead to his chin with my fingertips, I too decided that the things that happened needed to be remembered, but only in this book.

Those dark days needed to be put away for the time ahead. For our future together with our children. We had a wedding to attend and a realm to regain. Dwelling on Dylan's death and Levi's torture wouldn't get me anywhere. Now that I knew what had happened, it was abundantly clear why Levi hadn't told me. Part of it was his own struggle with his decisions while there. The other part was he wanted to protect me from the horrors that he and Dylan faced.

"Thank you for saving my daughter. Thank you for loving Dylan. Thank you for coming home to me." My voice cracked, and he kissed me gently.

"I will always come home to you," he replied.

Levi's story about his experiences in the Otherworld will be part of the Short Story Anthology that I will release in the fall of 2019. The story is called, *A Month of Sundays*.

CHAPTER ONE

"You've got to be kidding me," I said, looking at myself in the mirror. My *girlfriends* stood behind me giggling. They were all officially disowned. This white tulle and taffeta monstrosity was utterly ridiculous.

"I think it's gorgeous," Ella gushed. She and Astor had come through a portal this morning to help with wedding planning. He had whisked Levi off to do "man" things. I didn't want to know.

"It's too much. I can conjure a dress," I protested.

"You will not!" Jenny said.

"I agree. You need a proper, royal wedding dress, Grace," Betty added.

Jenny, Betty, Kady, Wendy, and Riley had arrived not long after Ella appeared. Ella looked ripe. It was only a matter of time, and she would pop out those twins. I could very clearly feel their presence. I also knew it was one boy and one girl. They had decided that they didn't want to know, and Levi made me swear not to tell.

"So, what kind of cake?" Riley asked. She sat in the recliner with a notepad and pen, writing down everything we *needed* for a proper royal wedding. I still wasn't sold on the idea of a huge wedding. Levi wanted one though. I could see the hurt in his eyes when I suggested we just elope.

"I don't care," I said.

"Grace! Are you really going to be bridezilla for the next two days?" Kady asked.

"I'm not a dinosaur, although I'm old enough to be one. Seriously though, this is not my idea of an ideal wedding. I'm only doing this for Levi," I said.

"And Levi would love to see you in that dress," Riley said.

If I had rolled my eyes any harder they would have jumped out the back of my head.

"This is too much," I repeated. "Something...less, please."

"Fine. Let's try this one," Wendy said, unzipping another of the five or six bags that Jenny had brought when she arrived. Tennyson apparently had connections in the wedding dress industry, as well. I shouldn't have been surprised.

"These would look better on you," I told Jenny.

"Um, no," she said. "I've been married."

"To my dad," I said. The chatter in the room silenced. "Step-mom," I added. Betty started giggling and the rest followed. Jenny watched me with a grin on her face. Thankfully, she wasn't mad.

I tucked my urge to rage at this whole process away. Humor was my disguise. For Levi.

"Oh, Grace! This one has blue in it. It would look great with your eyes," Wendy gushed. She didn't seem the type to let wedding dresses turn her into a girly girl, but apparently every woman had a soft spot for a wedding dress.

"Blue dress," I muttered as the memory flared to life in my head.

"You are wearing a long, blue dress that flows as the breeze blows around us."

Dylan's dream. I wondered if the dress was different when he dreamed about Levi and me. I pushed back the emotions, and thankfully, I was saved by the queen.

Chaz burst through the front door. "Oh, my stars, that is atrocious. Take that off," he said. I already had the taffeta mountain halfway off.

"Thank the heavens someone with taste is here." He leaned over and kissed Ella's belly gently.

"Hello, Charles," Ella said.

"Good grief," he huffed. "Please do not call me that in public. It ruins my image."

"We all know your name is Charles," Betty informed him.

"It's not the knowing. It's actually acknowledging the fact that I once was a stuffy twat of a man," he said.

"And now what are you?" I asked.

"Fabulous, of course." He saw Wendy with the white and blue dress in her hands. "Yes! Child, this is it. Put it on. Let me see." He clapped his hands, then sat down on the couch.

"Where is Winnie?" Jenny asked.

"Callum and Aydan took her into town to pick out a dress for the wedding. Callum mentioned picking up suits, too," I said.

"Too bad I'm not there to advise on that. Thankfully, Callum has taste," Chaz said.

"It doesn't matter what they wear," I said.

"I beg your pardon, but it does, Grace Ann Bryant. This is a royal wedding. If we had time, I'd make you watch the most recent royal wedding in England. You need a little refinement. You've lived in the trailer park too long," Chaz said.

"Thanks!" I replied.

"It wasn't a compliment," he huffed.

Wendy opened the bottom of the dress up and put it over my head. It slid down around me, falling into a less offensive bottom. The top was nice with lace and blue beading. It wasn't completely blue which I liked.

"That's it," Riley said.

"I agree," Kady added.

"You look beautiful, Grace," Betty said with a tear in her eye.

"That settles it," Jenny said. "This is your wedding dress."

"What?! Wait! Don't I get a say in the matter?" I asked.

"No!" they all shouted back at me.

"Geez, calm your tits," I grumbled.

When I looked in the mirror, I agreed. Levi would love it.

* * *

AFTER THEY DECIDED what dress I would wear, I let them decide on the other stuff, too. I had no idea all these things were needed for a wedding. Cake, flowers, reception food, etc.

"Where are you having the wedding?" Riley asked.

"I don't know," I said.

"There was a big house with a long front porch that wrapped around the side of the house. Behind it, there was a garden and a gazebo."

"Have it here in the garden," Riley suggested.

"No!" I said too loudly.

Stares.

"What's going on, honey?" Betty asked.

"Nothing. We can have it in town. In the town square," I said.

"The square is pretty damaged from the faun attack," Kady said.

"Oh," I replied, trying to think of anywhere but here.

"What about at the church?" Wendy suggested.

"No, that's Summer realm. It wouldn't be good for a Winter Queen to get married there," Ella explained.

"We will have it out at the stone circle," Jenny said. "Grace?"

"Yes," I replied. "That's good."

"Great. That's settled. Who's marrying you?" Riley asked.

"Matthew," I replied. I didn't care if that part of the dream was the same. Matthew had been the spiritual leader in the community for a long time. He had always been kind to me.

"He would love to do it," Kady said. "I'll let him know."

"Thank you," I replied.

"Alright. Who's giving you away?" Riley asked.

"Um, I dunno. Nestor, I guess."

"I know that Finley would like the job," Riley said.

"He would?"

"Yes. He said something about it this morning. He said it was his duty and that way if Levi messed up, he could kick his ass," Riley said with a smile.

"Oh, there will be a line for that if Levi messes up," Betty said.

"Leave him alone," I said, protecting my groom. "Levi has never done anything to harm me. He never will."

"Listen to that," Betty said.

"It sounds like love to me," Chaz added.

"We *are* getting married," I said.

"The gypsies would like to provide the music for the reception," Wendy said.

"Oh, good!" Riley replied, hastily writing it down in her notebook.

"I'm making the cake," Betty said. "And Luther said he had some other items for reception food."

"Like what?" I asked.

"You will see," she replied with a devious grin.

I saw splashes of gravy in my future.

"Tennyson has taken care of all the rental needs. Chairs, tables, etc."

"Chaz and I will make the bouquets. We just need to know what kind of flowers you want. It's late spring, so we can get just about anything here or in summer that you would want," Ella said.

"I don't really have a favorite. I'll defer to your expertise," I said.

"Grace, you've got to find something about this wedding and make it personal to you. If you don't, you'll regret it," Betty said. "This day is important, not just for you, but for all of us. The new monarchy is rising. The future of our people, and forgive me, if I want it to be amazing."

I hung my head. "There are just so many other things going on right now."

"This wedding will be the most important thing happening on this planet tomorrow. I can almost guarantee it. This is a promise to keep the veil intact. A promise to protect our people and the humans. You are marrying Levi, but the both of you represent what we all will become," she explained. "So, get with the program."

"Oh! Programs," Riley said, as she scribbled in her book again.

Betty's words took root. I'd never thought of it as anything more than pledging myself to Levi for the rest of eternity. She was right. This wedding meant a lot more than that. A hell of a lot more.

"You're right," I conceded. "It's just not who I am to get caught up in these things."

"Perhaps you should. Just this once," Chaz suggested. "It would mean a lot to all of us."

"I'll try."

CHAPTER TWO

"Well, you survived it," Levi said, as I recapped the planning session.

"I did, but I don't know how much longer I could talk about flowers and cake," I groaned. He laughed on the other end of the phone. "Where are you?"

"With Tennyson," he said.

"Where are you?" I repeated.

"Taking care of my part of the wedding stuff," he replied.

"Levi Rearden," I fussed.

"What? You callin' it off?" he asked.

"You know I'm not," I replied.

"Then you know what you need to know," he said.

"There better not be strippers involved," I said.

"And what if there are?" he teased.

"Levi!"

He just laughed instead of answering me, so I hung up on him.

"I love you, Grace."

"Nope. Not talking to you."

Then, he laughed in my head. Bastard bard.

I took a deep breath while stowing my phone in my pocket. I

needed to make this visit, but I knew it would hurt. I lightly tapped on the door and waited.

"Come on in. It's open," Remington Blake said.

I eased into his cabin that he once shared with Tabitha Mistborne. He sat in the corner, bruised and battered.

"Hey, Remy."

"Well, hello, Beautiful. Come sit with me. Forgive me if I don't get up."

"You don't have to. Not for me," I said.

"Grace, you can punish yourself for this all you want, but this was my fuck up. Not yours."

"I was so blind," I said.

"Hell, I was, too." He took a sip of his drink. I knew Remy, and I knew it was brandy. I slipped my hand into his free one. He squeezed it. "Stop worryin'. I'm gonna be fine."

"What can I do for you?" I asked.

"Nothing. I just need some time to sort it all out. I'll be at the wedding."

"Remy, you don't have to do that."

"Gracie, to see you settle down with one man! Hell, I'd pay good money for that, and now I get to see it for free," he teased. "I'll glamour all this up before I come."

He had bruises all over his body. Both of his eyes were black. Tennyson had talked to him and reported back to Levi that Tabitha had turned him over to her mother when the good doctor decided to make her move to be the heir to Summer. Apparently, it was part of Rhiannon's payment. My capture was part of it, too. Rhiannon had planted Tabitha in Shady Grove years ago hoping to find a way to get to my father's throne. When I moved to town, she had Tabitha befriend me. She also had her seduce Remington to keep me from going back to him. She wanted me with Dylan, because she knew she had ways to manipulate him with Stephanie. It was all very messed up. All three of them were dead, but during Remy's stay with Rhiannon, she used him as a punching bag. She never gave him any rhyme or reason, but he attributed it to his previous marriage with Phoebe and how he'd gotten out of it. Tennyson had worked that deal out without Rhiannon's knowledge. With Phoebe, who was Rowan, dead, Rhiannon took her frustration out on Remy without saying a word.

"You are a good man, Remington Blake," I said.

"I'm a liar and a cheat," he replied.

"I think we've all done bad things along the way, but right now, in this moment, you are righteous."

He chuckled, then sipped his brandy. "Righteous. Heh. I don't feel righteous."

"Has Wendy come to check on you?"

"She has. She's a nice lady. She brought Artemis with her this afternoon. Both very nice ladies. They are taking good care of me."

"What can I do?"

He looked at me with a crooked smile. "Grace Ann Bryant, you go get married and be happy. Even if it's just one damn day, be fucking happy. Dance and love. Because the battle to take Winter might kill us all," he said.

"You aren't fightin' in that battle."

"You gonna stop me?" he asked.

"Remy, what are you going to do?"

"Don't insult me after you just got finished bein' so sweet," he drolled.

"I'm sorry. I didn't mean it like that."

"Yeah, ya did. That's okay though, because you're right. I don't do much, but I can do something. Tennyson said he has a job for me. Niles is here to help."

"What is the job?" I asked.

"I don't know yet. He hasn't told me," he replied.

I sighed. Tennyson and his plans. He always had something up his sleeves. Both of them. I stood up, then leaned over Remy to kiss him on the forehead.

"Thank you, Remy."

"Whatcha thanking me for?"

"There was once a time when love was a concept I wouldn't even consider. You made me consider it. We got it wrong, but you opened a door that I thought I'd bolted shut. I wouldn't be getting married tomorrow if it weren't for you," I said.

"Levi is one lucky bastard," he said with a smile.

"Yes, he is."

"You are so very welcome, Gracie."

The door to the cabin opened, and Niles Babineau came in on the end of our conversation.

"My Queen! It is good to see you," he said with a slight bow.

"Hello, Niles," I said.

A young boy and girl followed him into the room.

"Grace, I'd like you to meet my children. This is my son, Kyrie, and my daughter, Celestina," Niles said. Both of the children beamed with a supernatural radiance.

"It is a pleasure to meet you," I said.

"Are you the queen?" Celestina asked.

"I am," I replied.

"I want to be a queen, too," she replied.

"Maybe one day you will be one," I said. "Niles, you are Star Folk, too?"

He nodded, but Remy explained. "Niles' influence reaches further than mine does. His gifts are stronger than mine. His children are a reflection of his power."

The boy leaned against the wall, staring at me. He seemed a bit aloof, but I didn't fault him. Meeting new people probably wasn't his thing. He looked to be about Winnie's age.

"How old are you, Kyrie?" I asked.

"My name is Kyrie Sterling Babineau," he said.

"Kyrie, you are being rude," Niles hissed.

"My sister's name is Celestina Azure Babineau. We are the children of the chief of the Star Folk. You rule below. We rule above," Kyrie said.

I lifted an eyebrow at Niles who cringed, then I died laughing. "This kid. I like him. Reminds me of someone I used to know."

"I can see that," Remy said.

"You, hush. I didn't ask you," I prodded at Remy.

He laughed, but Niles still looked uncomfortable. "Grace, I'm sorry. I've just tried to teach him to have pride in his heritage."

I waved his explanation off. "Niles, I'm not offended. Not in the least. You shall be treated like visiting dignitaries. Kyrie, I'm pleased to have your father and the both of you here to visit. Your father is right to teach you to have pride in your people. But you are a visitor in my kingdom. There is a difference between pride and being prideful. Being prideful will get you turned into dust." I snapped my finger, and Remy's glass of brandy turned into icy dust.

"Aw, Grace. Now I gotta get another glass," Remy whined.

Niles chuckled, but I saw the look in Kyrie's eyes. He'd gotten the point.

"Sorry, Niles," I said. "I'm just teaching him a little respect for his elders."

Celestina didn't flinch. She stared at me with wondrous eyes. Kyrie held his ground, but I saw the doubt creeping into his confident demeanor. I patted him on the shoulder. "Little lord, you are welcome here. I offer you all the hospitality that Shady Grove has to give. I meant it when I said I liked you, but I wished when I was your age, someone would have snapped a few glasses into oblivion for me."

"Yes, ma'am. Thank you," he replied sweetly. He still had the devil in his eyes though. Niles had his hands full with this one.

"You are welcome too, Miss Celestina," I said, offering her my hand.

"My friends call me Celeste," she said.

"Can I call you Celeste?" I asked.

"Yes, please," she replied.

"Well, good. Now see, Niles, we are all friends."

"I see," he replied. "I'll walk you out."

"Why thank you. Remy, I meant what I said." He huffed at me but didn't respond. I didn't want him fighting in this battle. He'd suffered enough.

Niles walked out to the truck with me. I knew he had something he wanted to say. I just wasn't sure who he didn't want to hear it.

"Grace, I would like my children and I to be allowed to stay in

Shady Grove. I still have holdings in New Orleans, but I've moved the majority of my business here. Most of what I do now is for Tennyson. It would help me to be closer to him," he requested.

"I don't have a problem with that. And I really do like your children," I said.

"Ah, yes, well, Kyrie is beginning to be a handful. Their mother isn't around much," he said.

"How is it that the Lord of the Star Folk has an estranged wife?" I asked.

"Just like any other man who has an estranged wife, I suppose. She found better things to do than raise her children," he said.

"You are doing a good job with them," I said.

"Only time will tell," he replied.

"How much influence do you have over Remy?" I asked.

"He's my subject as much as we are all yours."

"Make him stay here. I don't want him in the Otherworld."

"I'm not sure I can do that. He's pretty determined to do right by you."

"He's done more right by me than I can ever repay. I love that man in there. Not like I loved Dylan, and certainly not like I love Levi. But I don't want him to suffer any longer," I said.

"Well, if that little wolf doctor keeps coming around, I'd say you won't have to worry about him suffering too much." Niles laughed.

"Oh, really? I figured he'd be done with doctors."

"Remington Blake will never be done with women. No matter what profession."

I laughed in response. "That does make me feel better. Just take care of him for me."

"As you wish, my Queen," Niles said with a slight bow. He had the same smooth demeanor as Remy. I didn't know if that was tied to their Star Folk heritage or to their home, New Orleans. I did know that both of them were charmers. Which meant, little mister Kyrie was a charmer, too. I made a note to keep him away from Winnie.

CHAPTER THREE

I WANTED TO STOP BY HOT TIN AND GET NESTOR'S OPINION ON WHO should walk me down the aisle. Last thing I wanted to do was piss off the kelpie, especially after he'd smacked Levi down. I had to admit though I'd like to have seen him in all his shifted glory.

As I approached the bar, two figures stood holding hands in the middle of the street. I gripped the steering wheel because I couldn't believe what I was seeing. The two women looked to be lost and didn't move when I drove up to them.

I jumped out of the car. My tattoo flared sending blue streaks across my body. No mercy for traitors.

"Stephanie! Tabitha! What the fuck are you doing here?" I screamed at them. Both women fell to their knees. "That's not going to help you."

"Please, my Queen, we are here to serve you," Stephanie said.

A sparkling circle appeared to my right and Levi stepped through.

"Grace! Hold up!" Levi said.

"Hold up? Hold up? What the fuck, Levi?" I said, as he moved between the women and me.

"I promised Lilith to protect Stephanie," he said.

"Why the hell would you do that?" I asked.

"Because this is her second life. She's cursed to live in the veil. She does not remember anything," he explained.

"And Tabitha?"

"I don't know, but since she is here with her then she probably doesn't remember either," Levi said, turning to the women. "Tabitha, do you know why you are here?"

"The goddess said I should stay with Stephanie. She said that the king and queen of the vale would accept us," Tabitha whimpered, watching me through Levi's legs.

Levi slowly turned back to me. "I promised, Grace."

"I'm just supposed to look at the both of them every fucking day?" I protested.

Nestor stepped out of the bar with Aydan and Callum.

"Mom?" Aydan ran to me.

"Grace, what's going on?" Nestor asked.

"Ask Levi," I said, pointing at my fiancé.

"I promised Lilith that I would protect Stephanie when she returned to Shady Grove. I didn't know Tabitha would be part of the deal, but here she is," Levi explained.

"Their memories?" Nestor asked.

"Are wiped," Levi responded.

"Grace, this is how this works. In your second life, you get to choose whether to remember or not. If they are exiles, you are their Queen," Nestor explained.

"I don't want to be their Queen!"

"You don't get to choose your subjects sometimes, Grace. They are part of the vale now," Nestor said.

I lowered my hand, allowing my power to fade. "When were you going to tell me about this?" I asked Levi.

"A lot happened, Grace. And we've rushed right into this wedding. I had no idea it would be now anyway," he explained. "I'm sorry. It was something important that slipped. I would never hide anything from you on purpose."

"Likely story," Aydan said.

"Aydan," I scolded him.

Levi grinned at him, then approached me slowly. "They could prove to be very powerful allies. They don't remember anything."

"They betrayed us. Both of them. We almost lost Tennyson. We lost your father," I countered.

He made it to me, wrapping his arms around my waist. I stood stiffly, ignoring him the best I could. "Levi."

He planted a soft kiss on my cheek. "Grace."

"Anything else you need to tell me?"

"I love you."

"Cop out."

"That's twice today that I've told you that I loved you, and you've ignored me. Don't make me prove it," he whispered in my ear.

Aydan had backed off giving us some room.

"Get away from her!" Jenny said, stepping out of the bar.

Levi growled, then looked back over to her.

"I mean it! Go back to the men. She's got a party to attend. Take the boys with you," Jenny told Levi.

"I'm in the middle of something, Jenny," Levi said.

"I don't care. You will have her tomorrow," she replied. "What are they doing here?"

"Second life," Nestor said.

"Oh, hell," Jenny grumbled. "I'll call Tennyson and get them somewhere to stay. Put a guard on them for now."

"Their memories are erased," Nestor replied.

Jenny lifted the phone to her ear. "Still, fairies."

"Agreed," I said.

"Grace," Levi prompted.

"What?"

He grinned like a fool. His blue eyes sparkled with humor and love. I was a lucky fairy, but it was so hard to let him win. He already knew what he did to me. Why should I give him more? I was giving him a big, fat wedding.

"Grace," he practically sang my name. His power rippled over my skin in goosebumps. It wasn't a command. Just a reminder.

"I love you, Levi."

"Was that so hard?" he teased.

"I'm only concerned with one hard thing," I replied.

"Okay, enough of that," Jenny said, grabbing my arm. "Come on. Levi, Stone and Bronx are coming for the women. You get the boys to Tennyson's place."

"Yes, ma'am," he responded, keeping his eyes on me.

I shook my head, as Jenny dragged me into the Hot Tin Roof Bar.

CHAPTER FOUR

"Surprise!" The bar erupted in noise.

"What is this?" I asked.

White streamers and balloons filled the bar and hung off all the light fixtures. A large pink cake sat on the bar surrounded by strawberry margaritas. Ella ,with her giant belly, sat on one of the stools next to a pile of presents. Mrs. Frist stood behind the counter with a towel over her shoulder. Chaz, Betty, and Wendy stood next to each other at the jukebox. Artemis and Amanda sat at one of the tables.

Riley walked up to me with a fake crown with a veil, then positioned it on my head. "There. Here comes the bride," she said.

"You are having entirely too much fun with this," I said.

"It's not every day we get to have a royal wedding," Jenny said.

Brittany Arizona, my tattoo artist, and Juanita Santiago were there, too. Even the waitress from the BBQ place, Tonya, sat with the other ladies at a table.

"Is this a bachelorette party?" I asked.

"Sort of. It's a mix between a bridal shower and a bachelorette party," Jenny said. "It was Riley's idea."

"Yes! So, have a drink," she said, handing me a margarita. "And open your presents."

"I don't need presents. I have everything I need," I said.

"It's wedding tradition. Open your presents, Grace!" Mrs. Frist said.

"Why are you behind Nestor's bar?" I asked.

"He allowed me to do it," she said with a smirk.

"Oh, hell," I grumbled. My grandfather had rolled out of the snake's bed and into the spider's.

"Here open this one," Jenny said, setting one down in front of me. The women gathered around me as I began to open the presents. Standard wedding presents. A mixer. Silver photo frame. Waffle maker. Bottles of wine.

I sat among the gifts, chatting with the women when Jenny placed one last present in front of me. She sat a bottle of my favorite whiskey next to it.

"You are going to need that," she said.

"Who is this from?" I asked, smiling at the ladies.

"Levi," Jenny answered.

"What?" I asked. My curiosity peaked, and I opened the small package. "Oh!" The sound came out more like a whimper than anything.

Reaching into the package, I pulled out a delicate rose-covered teacup. The women made a collective sappy moan. Inside the box, I found a small envelope. I unfolded the paper while holding back tears.

"Well, read it for all of us," Chaz insisted while wiping a tear with a silk handkerchief.

"Um, okay." I tried finding my voice.

GRACE,

It took me forever to find the exact one, but I finally did. When I was in the Otherworld with Dylan, he asked about the cup. I told him that it probably went down with the trailer. He wanted me to make sure I found another one to remind you of what you meant to him. I assured him that you would never forget him. The more I thought about it, I realized how important that cup was to me, too. Dylan's love melted your heart. Helped you to find your-

self once again. And I couldn't be more grateful to him for it. Without him, I wouldn't have you. So, here is your teacup. Pour a little whiskey in, and toast to Dylan.

All my love,
Levi

I OPENED the whiskey and poured some in the cup.

"To Dylan," I said.

The ladies in the room lifted their glasses and echoed, "To Dylan."

"Damn, Levi," I muttered. Betty leaned over and kissed me on the temple.

"I agree. Damn, Levi. This was supposed to be a fun time! Riley, don't we have some entertainment?" Betty asked.

"We do!" Riley said, perking up. She dragged a chair across the room over to the pool table. "Come on, Grace. You get the seat of honor." She patted the seat. I shook my head reminding myself that I was doing all of this for Levi.

Levi.

"Thank you."

"Are you crying?"

"No. Maybe."

"You are welcome. Have fun."

"You, too. But no strippers."

"Hey! I didn't plan this."

"Are there strippers?"

"Not yet." He sounded disappointed. Men.

I sighed, then took a seat in the chair.

"Everything okay?" Jenny asked, knowing I was talking to Levi.

"He won't tell me if there are strippers."

"Did someone say strippers?" Wendy asked.

She opened the bar door, and Cletus and Tater stepped inside with a boom box. Tater sat it down on the table and grinned at me.

"Oh, my goddess," I mumbled.

Jenny and Riley giggled as Nelly's *Hot in Herre* began to blast out of the speakers.

In all of my years, I'd never seen what happened next. Tater and Cletus began twisting and jerking around all the women who whooped and hollered. Betty stuck dollar bills in Cletus' overalls while Tater jiggled his butt in front of Ella. She backed away from him laughing, but Chaz slapped him on the ass. Tater yelped but kept dancing. I shook my head as he started toward me. When I tried to stand up, Riley forced me back down into the chair.

Cletus unlatched his overalls allowing them to sink to the ground. He was wearing a pair of boxers that said, "Redneck Romeo." He shimmied his way toward me with two golden teeth shining from his mouth. I laughed because I couldn't cry.

Tater wobbled behind him.

"Lookie at my new pants, Grace!" he yelled, grabbing the waist band. He pulled and the snaps up the legs gave way revealing his tighty-whities. "Ain't that cool!"

"Um, yeah," I whimpered.

The two goofballs danced around me, twerking things that shouldn't be twerked. I was going to kill Riley. She stood back clapping and laughing. Then, I saw it. Mrs. Frist held up a cell phone recording the whole thing.

"Put that phone up!" I said.

"No way, my Queen. I have dirt on all the monarchs," she laughed. I almost thought she was joking, but I knew better.

"Levi is going to die," I screamed to Riley.

"Levi knew," she responded with a wink.

"Have mercy," I muttered as Cletus' ass wiggled in my face.

Thankfully, they didn't invest in the extended version of Nelly's song and after four minutes of vomit-inducing hilarity, Cletus and Tater gathered their garments and excused themselves from the party.

"Wasn't that fun?" Betty said.

"You guys are nuts," I exclaimed. "Really?"

"Well, it's hard to get a stripper at short notice out in a town that technically no longer exists. Although, a guy named Seamus called and volunteered," Riley said.

"I might have liked that," I said.

"Grace!" Jenny scolded.

"You've seen him. He's good looking for a vamp."

"Pirate."

"Vampirate."

"I'd like to meet him," Mrs. Frist said.

"You would," I replied. "So, what's next?"

"Shots!" Riley exclaimed.

Mrs. Frist produced a tray of whiskey shots. She handed an empty glass to Ella, then filled it with sweet tea.

"Everyone take one," Betty instructed.

The women of my town gathered around the tray. Each one took a shot holding it in their hands. I took the last one and lifted it to throw it back.

"Nope. Hold up," Riley said. "We each have something to say."

"Me, first!" Amanda said. "Thank you, Grace, for not killing me. For allowing me to stay in Shady Grove. I've never been happier in all my life."

"You are welcome," I said.

"Grace, thank you for saving me from a terrible marriage. For making me a part of this town and taking care of my family," Juanita said.

"You should be thanking me for all the times I listened to your sad stories," Chaz said. "But since this isn't about me, thanks for hooking my daughter up with the best knight."

"Hey! That's my thank you!" Ella exclaimed.

"Too bad," Chaz smirked.

We laughed at them, but the thanks continued.

"Thank you, Grace, for trusting me even when we didn't see eye to eye," Betty said, then elbowed Mrs. Frist.

"Oh, um, thanks for tolerating me," she said.

I laughed. "You're welcome."

"Thank you for allowing the gypsies to stay here under your

protection despite your past connection with Fordele. We feel like we are at home here," Wendy said.

I nodded to her. But they continued.

"Thank you for helping deliver three beautiful little girls when I was in over my head," Artemis said.

"Thanks for saving Brad last Christmas. I don't know what I'd do without my boss," Tonya said.

"He just your boss?" I asked.

She grinned. "No."

"You go, girl," I said, offering her a fist bump which she returned.

"It's an honor to know that my art is on the Queen and King's arm. I know now how important those tattoos are. I'm thankful to have been a small part of it," Brittany said.

"You do good work," I said.

"I'm also the only tattoo artist in town," she said with a smile.

"That helps," I said. "But you did my tattoo before you moved here."

"I did," she said. "You and a bunch of women from a trailer park."

"It seems like it was so long ago," I said.

"It's been seven years," Brittany replied.

"Thank you, Brittany."

"My pleasure," she said.

Everyone faced Riley who hadn't spoken yet. She looked down at her shot glass, then back up to me. "I'm very happy for you and Levi. I'm also very proud to be a Bryant."

"What?!"

"Finley and I went to see Judge Chastain this afternoon and eloped. He didn't want to do this whole wedding thing," she said, showing us her wedding band.

"I've never had a sister," I said.

"You may regret having one now," she said.

"No, if you make Finley happy, then you are the best sister I could ask for," I said, lifting my shot glass. "To family. Because you all thank me for these things, and it means a lot to me. But you are my family."

"Even Frist?" Betty asked. Mrs. Frist kicked her.

"Even Frist. To family," I repeated.

"To family!" they echoed, then pounded back the whiskey.

"Damn that's strong shit," I said.

"You are a lightweight," Betty teased.

"Maybe I am now. I'm a mom," I replied.

"And you are going to be a wife," Amanda said. "Good luck with that."

"I'm gonna need it," I admitted.

.

CHAPTER FIVE

T<small>ROY</small> <small>SHOWED UP AT THE BAR SHORTLY AFTER ALL THE WOMEN</small> dispersed, except for Mrs. Frist who washed dishes behind the bar like she owned it. I couldn't wait to ask Nestor about that.

"Were you surprised?" Troy asked.

"Very," I replied, as Winnie barreled out of the car and hugged me. "Hey, pumpkin, did you have fun with Mark?"

"No," she replied. "Mark doesn't like me anymore."

Troy laughed uncomfortably. "He's going through some changes."

"Alpha changes?" I asked.

"Yeah," Troy replied. "He's very engaged with the pack now. When he's not out with the guys, he's watching over his sisters. He will grow out of it."

"It's okay. Just a fact of life. Winnie will be fine. Won't you?" I asked.

"I'm fine without that stupid boy," she huffed.

"Sounds like her momma," Amanda said.

"Shut it," I replied. "Maybe a little."

"Can we go home?" Winnie asked.

"Yes, ma'am. Amanda, where was Kady tonight?" I asked.

"She wanted to spend the evening with Caleb and Matthew," she said.

"Ah. Okay," I replied.

Winnie chattered all the way home. She was disappointed with Mark's lack of attention, but she loved playing with the babies.

"Are you going to have another baby?" she asked.

"I don't know, Winnie. You know we have a big battle coming up," I said.

"I don't like when you have to fight, but I know why you do," she said.

"Why do I?" I asked.

"Because you are a good person," she said.

"I try, baby," I said.

"Besides, you are going to win," she said.

"Oh yeah? How do you know that?"

"I saw it in a dream."

I pulled the truck over to the side of the road.

"A dream?"

"Yes, I had a dream that you were standing in front of a bunch of fairies, and it was cold. Uncle Levi was with you, and you both were wearing crowns," she said.

"When did you have this dream?"

"I've had it a couple of times. I like it because I'm wearing a long pretty dress like the one I bought for the wedding."

Was it possible that Winnie was having future dreams like Dylan? Part of her Phoenix traits developing? Dylan had warned me that the dreams change, but for now, Winnie believed we would win the war. I couldn't wait to tell Levi, but decided it was something better told in person.

I continued on my way thinking I was returning to a quiet house, but from the looks of it, something had happened. Levi and Tennyson stood on the front porch, and shadows moved around inside the house past the windows. LeAnne, the Valkyrie, stood on the porch like a statue. Her presence comforted me in a way, but she was different. Very dedicated to her task.

Climbing out of the truck, I asked, "What's wrong?"

Winnie ran up to Levi who threw her up over his head, then placed her back on the ground. She giggled, then ran into the house.

"Astor received word from Summer that Winter troops were patrolling the border near the tree," Levi said.

"What? Who is out there?" I asked.

"Joey Blankenship is the new knight of the tree," Tennyson explained. "He sent word."

"This wedding is a mistake," I said.

"It will happen, Grace. You and Levi have to be married. We can't take any chances," Tennyson insisted.

"Connie went to check the border at the fountain," Levi said. "And the wedding is a mistake?"

"Not marrying you. Just us being distracted with bridal showers," I said.

"And strippers," Levi grinned.

"What strippers?"

"I saw the video," he laughed.

"Frist," I growled.

"Finley, Astor, Nestor, and the boys are inside," Levi said, as Tennyson left us alone.

"I'm sorry. I didn't mean it like that, Levi."

He tugged my arm and I gave into him, curling into his arms. "I know you didn't."

"Winnie had a dream."

He stepped back to face me. "A dream?"

"I think it was like Dylan's dreams."

A worried look crossed his face. "What was the dream?"

"She dreams of us as King and Queen of Winter," I said.

He rubbed my cheek with his thumb. "Isn't that what we are fighting for?"

"Yes, but how is she having dreams? Dylan only had them drunk."

"That's because that was the only time that Dylan lost control. He fought to control his abilities. To use them when he wanted, how he wanted. That included the dreams. Winnie hasn't mastered that control yet."

"I know. It worries me."

"Why? She has the best momma in the world."

"You are a sweet talker, Levi Rearden."

"I'm gonna ask Cletus where he got those boxers."

I poked him in the side, then rushed to the door. He put his arm up in front of it before I went in. "I know you like me better in nothing at all."

"Would you stop? The freaking fairies are threatening the borders," I said, getting frustrated.

"And we can't do anything at the moment, so I might as well tease my future wife," he said.

"Get out of my way!"

The Valkyrie never moved or even looked at us while we flirted with each other. Her eyes remained on the drive back to the main road.

"Well, don't go pitchin' a hissy fit." He opened the door for me. "Welcome home, my Queen."

"I'm going to jerk a knot in your tail," I whispered, walking past him into the house.

"Hot damn," he said.

"Grace, glad you are here," Tennyson said.

"Well, yes, this is my house," I replied.

"It is. I never questioned that," he said.

"I do. Regularly," I replied. Levi poked me in the back. With his finger. Not the appendage I'd hoped for.

"We are waiting for word from my son about the fountain border," he said.

"We aren't equipped to defend both the tree and the fountain at the same time," I said.

"And he isn't equipped to attack them both at the same time. Astor has moved the new knights of the tree closer to the tree, to show a presence. Galahad will instruct Edwin to beef up their patrols. I don't think he's poised to attack. Perhaps he's just trying to disrupt certain happenings here," Tennyson said.

"The wedding," I surmised.

"Yes," Tennyson said.

"We should elope like Finley," I said.

"Finley! You eloped?" Levi asked.

"Hell, yeah. No way I'm going through this pomp and monkey suits," Finley said, while lounging in my recliner.

"Congrats, by the way. Thanks for leaving us out of it," I said snidely.

"You are welcome. It was a beautiful, simple, quiet ceremony," Finley said.

I was jealous. It sounded perfect.

"Grace, don't get any ideas. Your wedding to Levi needs to be public, and big," Tennyson said. "The whole world needs to know that you and he are married. A force to be reckoned with. We are so close to taking back Winter. This is a step to that end."

"I know. I know," I said. "So, how long do we wait on Galahad?"

"I'm not sure, but I called Wendy. She is on the way. Finley called Riley who is going to pick up Kady on the way here. We might need their help if we have to split forces, and having the witches involved will help," Tennyson explained.

"So, we are in a holding pattern?" Levi asked.

"Essentially," Tennyson said.

"Good. Excuse us," Levi said, grabbing my hand and pulling me away from the group. He led me down the hallway to the room where Callum slept.

"What's going on?" I asked as he shut the door behind us.

"Did you have fun at the party?" he asked.

"Yes, and the teacup was too much."

"I debated on when to give it to you, but I thought with the support of the women there with you would be the best time," he said.

It always surprised me how big Levi's heart was, and how much love it contained. He gave me a gift that he knew would make me sad, but he also knew I needed it even if it had come from Dylan in the first place. I'd never understand how he was so intuitive of what I needed or wanted, but he always knew. He never hesitated to give it to me. From a teacup to bath bombs, Levi knew exactly what I needed and when. My heart inside him must have had something to do with it, but I didn't know how it was physically possible for such a thing to happen. It had happened. I knew it to be true from the moment he told me. It was almost as if I had always known from the first time I looked at him. In that moment, I thought that he was deep trouble or in it. Turned out to be both, and here I was in it with him.

"I never thought I'd ever see one like it again," I said.

He kissed me gently on my lips. "You still aren't on board for this wedding."

"I am on board for marrying you, but the wedding is too much. It's a distraction. This could be bad," I said.

"Stop worrying. We have everything under control. Just relax and walk down the aisle to me tomorrow, and once we are married, you can storm through Winter," he said.

"Well, it won't happen like that," I said.

"Then you can storm through me," he said.

I laughed. "That was lame."

"It was, but I'm grasping for straws here."

"Why do you want a big wedding?"

"Because you deserve it and you don't even realize it. You are a Queen, and yeah, I'm a King, but I wouldn't be anything without you. You deserve to have the attention of everyone in this town. You deserve a public declaration that I promise to be your partner for as long as we live. And I can't wait to strip you out of a wedding gown." He waggled his eyebrows.

"Dublin."

"Hmm?"

"I could just put it on now and we could."

"No! Don't ruin it!"

I sighed. "I'm doing this for you."

"Don't do it for me. Do it for us."

"I'd rather just do it for you."

"Aren't you sweet?" he teased.

"Sometimes I am," I protested.

"Don't let it become a habit."

"Or what?"

"I'll have to punish you," he said, unleashing a chord down his guitar. My knees wobbled.

"What the hell was that?"

"Just a sample of your wedding night."

"Why wait?"

Jenny barreled into the room without knocking. "Nope. Out! Now! No gravy swapping the night before the wedding."

"We weren't, Mom!" I protested.

She put her hands on her hips and pointed at the door.

"We're in trouble," Levi teased.

"Out!" Jenny demanded.

Levi and I giggled all the way back to the living room where Troy and Dominick had joined the group.

"Oh, who let the dogs out?" I said in my reverie. Levi snorted behind me, while Finley held his hand in front of his face.

"Hello, Grace," Dominick said with a grin.

"Hi," I replied with a twiddle of my fingers.

"Uncle Nick!" Winnie said, running up to Dominick.

"Uncle Nick?" I asked.

"Yes, Uncle Levi told me that Uncle Nick is my uncle too!" Winnie explained.

"Oh, really?" I said, looking at my groom.

"Can you have too many uncles?" Levi asked.

"I guess not," I said. "I'll fix some drinks for everyone while we wait."

"Alright. I'm going to get Troy caught up," Levi said.

I made my way to the kitchen, taking out glasses for everyone. Dominick joined me without my daughter around his neck.

"Well, hello, Uncle Nick."

"Levi's idea."

"Yeah, he told me. Grab that tea out of the fridge, will ya?"

He took out the tea and poured it into the glasses. Levi had told me how close they had become, and he felt like Dominick would be a big part of our lives. I knew how he felt, but I never wanted to express too much of that feeling. As much as I used to like the attention, I didn't want to give Dominick the wrong impression. I didn't want to give Levi the wrong impression either by telling him I thought Nick was special.

Nick wore the leather cuff that Levi had made for him. I looked at it through my sight. Outside of the tawny brown of Dominick's werewolf power, I saw the cool blue of Levi's ties to Winter. We knew that Nick was a Faeborn shifter, and that at some point, he would be able to tap those powers even though he had shunned it most of his life.

"It works pretty good," he said, catching me looking at the cuff.

"My man does good work," I said.

"He absolutely does, but I wouldn't have gotten to this point if you hadn't kicked me in the seat of my pants," Nick said.

"Well, I have a habit of being forceful and a pain in the butt," I replied.

"Yes, you do." We laughed. "I wouldn't change a thing about you, Grace. You are amazing."

"Why, thank you. You've been taking sweet talker lessons from Levi."

"Nah! I did that long before he came around."

"I believe it. Will you help me hand out these drinks?"

"Sure." He picked up several of them and moved around the room, offering them to our guests. When he got to the last one, he came back for more. Finally, he took the last one for himself and settled down next to Winnie who was coloring pictures on the coffee table. I sat down near them.

"Momma, Uncle Nick says that Mark will be my friend again someday," she said.

I looked at Nick who shrugged. "He's going through a phase. All young wolves do. Add the Alpha element, and you've got a mess on your hands. He means well, but he's not figured it all out yet."

"I can understand that. I've got my own little supernatural girl figuring things out," I said, brushing my hand through her dark brown hair. "She's dreaming and changing the color of her eyes. Who knows what power she will have one day?"

"I'm going to be like you," Winnie said.

"Lord have mercy," Levi said, sitting down next to me.

"What will you do with two of us?" I asked him.

"Lose my mind," he said.

"Good luck, brother," Nick said.

"Thanks. I'm gonna need it," Levi replied.

"You sure are," Winnie added.

We were laughing at her sassy innocence when Connelly returned. The room got quiet as he walked in the front door without knocking.

"Dad, they are just patrolling the borders. The forces are made of wild things. Lots of them," he said.

"I was afraid of that," Tennyson said.

"Afraid of what?" I asked.

"Demetris Lysander and Brockton were working together in the law firm to amass an army of wild things that had made their way into the human world, but had gotten caught. It's what started all of this, if you recall," Tennyson said.

"How could I forget?" I remembered the night that I gave Demetris Lysander's life to my father and almost killed Amanda for her participation in his scheme. It was the night I learned that Dylan was the Phoenix.

"They were trying to get rid of you, and almost succeeded multiple times. I didn't think they anticipated your father giving you Winter. With Lysander's death, the minions he'd established defaulted to Brockton. We've dug around and there are no less than a couple of thousand wild fairies that they've recruited to their cause. Once he moved them to the Otherworld, it would have been easy to recruit more. We aren't facing a Winter force. We are facing a Wild one," Tennyson explained.

In the depths of Winter, there is a low-lying mountain range covered in dense forest. It was forbidden for any Winter fairy to go there even though it fell within our realm. The beings who lived there were the worst of the worst of us. I'd been close to it before, and the whole vibe of the place reeked of darkness. I knew the darkness inside of me. Unbridled power. The feel of the Wild Lands, as they were called, made my darkness look like a beacon in a cold, dark winter night.

Once, when I was younger, I watched my father walk into the Wild Lands. He ruled them and occasionally he would go there to remind them of it. I'd never feared for my father's life, but that day I did. I sat in the carriage that had taken us to the border with my eyes glued to the spot where he had gone inside. The darkness seemed to hug him as he disappeared from my sight. I remember Finley thinking the place was cool, but I figured that was just bravado. It had to have scared him as much as it did me.

Father returned to us and did not speak on the way back to the castle. Just before we exited the carriage, he gave us a warning.

"Never go into the Wild Lands. If you go in, not even my crown can save you. The beasts inside will devour you. Do you understand?"

We nodded our heads. I remembered Finley boasting that he wasn't scared, but I knew him better than that. It spooked him as much as it had me.

Now those wild fairies were roaming the borders of Summer. We had to move quickly to take Winter. I hoped I had enough authority to send those beings back to their dark home or kill them if we had to. However, I worried that killing a large group of them might start a war between us and them. That would be a bigger war than the one we were currently fighting.

"Grace?" Levi nudged me.

"Huh?"

"Where did you go?" he asked.

"The Wild Lands and the creatures that live in them are extremely dangerous. If Brockton has truly allied with them, then we might have a much longer war ahead of us," I said. "One that would claim far more lives than we could imagine." I looked down at my daughter innocently coloring in her favorite book.

"We don't have any proof that he has allied with the whole of the wild fairies. Just those that he recruited through his law practice," Tennyson said.

"What happened to Kyffin Merrick?" Jenny asked.

"Kyffin was Brockton's partner at the firm. He's been missing since Brockton came here with Stephanie and killed your father. I have someone searching for him," Tennyson said.

"Perhaps he's the connection to the Wild?" I asked. "Who is he? Or, who was he?"

Tennyson's eyes darkened, and he wiped sweat from his brow with his pocket handkerchief. Jenny squeezed his shoulder in assurance.

"Kyffin Merrick is Gareth. Mordred's half-brother. I killed him and his brother," Tennyson said.

I knew the story. Lancelot had gone to save Guinevere and had killed the brothers Gareth and Gaheris in the process. Many stories said they were unarmed, but there were very few occasions when a knight was unarmed. It seemed impossible that the honorable Lancelot would have done such a thing. However, considering Guinevere was in trouble, he might have done anything to save her. Mordred had used the deaths to drive a wedge between Lancelot and Arthur along with exposing Lancelot's affair with the Queen. Of course, my father had known about the affair, but it had never been publicized until Mordred made his move for the throne.

"Do we know if he is alive? Any indications?" I asked.

"I believe that he is. One of my best assassins is on his trail. If she cannot find him, no one can," Tennyson explained.

"She?" Nick asked.

"Yes, she," Tennyson confirmed, but said no more about the woman.

"What do we do now?" I asked.

"Wait for him to make a move," Tennyson said. "And have a wedding."

"Hear, hear," Troy said, lifting his sweet tea. "To the biggest wedding this side of the Otherworld."

Those in the room lightheartedly clinked glasses, but the shadow of war hung heavily over the room. It would be hard to celebrate anything knowing that the next day we all might die.

CHAPTER SIX

Wendy arrived with Fordele in tow, and Riley arrived not much later with Kady who looked to be in a terrible mood. We gave them the run-down of the action at the borders. They agreed to help us in the event that Brockton made a move on either end.

"With Robin dead, the ORCs will replace her to fill their trinity," Wendy warned.

"Yes, but who?" I asked.

"I'd say that Lisette is probably more powerful than we thought or at least had a major upgrade since you last faced her," Kady supplied.

"I have to agree with that," Riley said.

"Do we have any possible ideas of who it might be?" I asked.

"I could see Tabitha or Stephanie stepping into the role, but with both of them dead, I don't know who else would," Riley answered.

I looked at Levi who nodded. "Stephanie and Tabitha are here in Shady Grove. Banished to the veil for their actions with their memories erased."

"What?!" Wendy exclaimed.

"I know. I almost dusted both of them," I said.

"Why didn't you?" Wendy asked.

"Because I swore to protect them," Levi said.

Riley laughed and Wendy shook her head.

"He's too good for his own good," I smirked.

"Lilith made me," he complained.

"No way out of that one," Wendy said, giving him a pass.

"It's okay. We have them under guard," Jenny supplied.

"They really are the least of our worries," I said.

"They might be helpful though. That kind of power on our side," Riley mused.

"Do they still have the powers of fairy queens?" I asked.

"I dunno," Riley said. "But if they did, that's a bonus for us. We just need to train them."

"Hold up a minute," Troy interrupted. "We can't put any trust in them until they have proven themselves. We can't take any chances."

"I agree," I said. "Maybe in the future, but not right now. Not with this."

We talked a while longer about strategies and how to defend two borders at once. Levi and I agreed that we might have to just choose the middle, but the ORCs had cut off our access directly to my father's castle by moving the exit of the portal at the hedge maze to the fountain. Very much like the tree's distance from the center of Summer, the fountain was a trek from it to the Winter stronghold.

"Can't we just move it back?" I asked.

"I've looked through Mable's book and I haven't found anything. I'm not sure how they moved it in the first place," Levi said.

"I can get us to the castle," Tennyson said flatly. No need to question that any longer. We'd learned Tennyson's voice, and he meant business about this. "We have a wedding to attend tomorrow, and it's time for this meeting to break-up. Levi, you are coming with me."

"Why?" I asked.

"You can see him tomorrow at the wedding," Jenny said.

"Aw, come on. It's not like we aren't already…" Levi put his hand over my mouth and looked at Winnie.

"That doesn't matter. It's tradition. Levi, go!" Jenny ordered.

"You can just skip back to my room later."

"And no skipping, I'm putting up a ward," Wendy said.

"You all hate me," I whined.

"Walk me to the door," Levi said, tugging my hand.

"Are you okay with this? It's bullying!"

"Stop being so dramatic," he teased, pulling me into his arms. His hand found that spot on my neck, and I melted into him. "I'll be in a tux tomorrow out at the circle waiting on you. Don't make me come and get you."

"I'll be there," I said. He leaned in brushing his lips against mine lightly. Teasing me. His hand tightened on my neck as he pressed into a deeper kiss. His tongue brushed over mine, driving the fairy inside of me insane.

"Ew!" Winnie exclaimed.

We broke the kiss with huge grins.

"Tomorrow," he said.

"Tomorrow," I replied.

Tennyson smiled more than his normal as he walked past Levi out the door. When Levi released me, my body begged for his to come back to me, but I sighed, knowing that so much depended on tomorrow. I saw the promise in his eyes to make it all worth it. I would hold him to it.

I said good-bye to all of our guests one by one as they left, but Jenny remained.

"You here to keep me honest?" I asked.

"Yep. I know Levi will follow the rules, but you won't," she said. "Just go upstairs. Put Winnie to bed, then come back down here."

"Not to bed?" I asked.

"Nope. We need to talk," she said.

"Um, okay." It sounded ominous, but I trusted her. "Winnie, bedtime little miss."

"Yes, ma'am," she said immediately. Normally she fought me on bedtime, but today she scooped up her crayons and books, then headed upstairs. I followed to her room where we picked out pajamas and she brushed her teeth.

She crawled into the bed, and I sat down next to her.

"I love you, Winnie," I said.

"I love you, too. Do you think Daddy will be watching the wedding tomorrow?"

"I don't know. What do you think?" I asked.

"I am going to wear my key so that he can watch. He loved Uncle Levi, too."

"Yes, he did. Just because I'm marrying Levi doesn't mean that I don't love Dylan anymore."

"Really?"

"Really. It's hard to explain, but your daddy will always be a part of me. I see him in you with your powers. I see him in your brother. He is always here with us."

"So, he will be there."

"Yeah," I replied.

"Good."

"Goodnight, my little wildfire."

I quietly backed out of the room, leaving her with Bramble and Briar who had emerged from the dollhouse to join Winnie on the bed. They waved at me as I shut the door. The two little brownies had been quiet lately with Thistle running errands for Tennyson. Thankfully, no new roleplaying, which Winnie called dress-up. Oh, to be innocent again.

I slipped into something comfortable, then went back downstairs to find Jenny sitting in the living room with a fresh pot of coffee brewing in the kitchen. Perhaps it was going to be a long night.

"Thanks for the bachelorette party," I said.

"I'm glad you had fun."

"I did. What is Nestor doing with Frist?" I asked.

"I'll let him answer that one, because honestly, I don't know," she said.

"So, a pot of coffee."

"Yeah, we need to talk about the Otherworld, and your rule in Winter. Tennyson had some concerns and he thought it would be best that I brought them up to you," Jenny said.

"Is something wrong?" I asked.

"Have a seat, and we will talk," she said, motioning to the other end of the couch.

I didn't know where this was going, and she had me concerned.

"Okay. Spill it."

"As soon as you and Levi are married, Aydan is no longer eligible for the throne," she said.

"We are getting married, so he doesn't have to worry about that," I said.

"And what if both of you die taking back Winter," she said.

"I can't pop a baby out in one day. I'm good, but I ain't that good," I said. "Can't I just appoint someone to take over for me or something?"

"No, you can't."

"My father got Winter from Mab. They weren't related," I said. She stared at me, and it hit me. "Fuck, fuck, fuck, fuck." I got up and paced the room. "So, was she his original mother or his fairy second life mother?" I asked.

"Both," she replied.

"I have to kill my grandmother who was sleeping with my grandfather," I said.

"Which is why Nestor has been a little upset once he figured out who she was," Jenny said.

"Why didn't he tell me?!"

"Because I asked him to allow me to do it. Titania's offspring was Morgana who became Rhiannon," she explained.

"I thought that Rhiannon and father were siblings," I said.

"Mab was Igraine, who had many children. Arthur by Uther and Morgana by her first husband, making your father and Morgana siblings. Then when they both passed from Camelot into Avalon, the Queens decided that they should split the Otherworld between the two siblings who sometimes loved each other and sometimes hated each other. They felt it was a perfect balance. Titania took Morgana's second life making her Rhiannon, her daughter."

"How was Mab here as Mable for so long and none of us knew who she was?" I asked.

"Mab was renowned for her glamours. No one here could have possibly known. Not even Nestor," she said.

"Nestor," I sighed. "No wonder it upset him."

"She turned on us, but learning her true identity hit him pretty hard."

"I was giving him room. I didn't want to push the issue."

"Which is what he wanted, but Tennyson can be less than caring about things sometimes. Which I also need to tell you that Tennyson interviewed Nestor and believes that he was innocent in all of it."

"Interviewed?! You mean interrogated!"

"No, interviewed with moonshine. Nestor did it willingly."

"I didn't need that kind of proof."

"I understand that, but we did."

"You shouldn't have."

"We were just watching out for your interests."

"From now on, when it comes to *my* family, you come to *me* first. Do you understand?" The blue Winter power in my veins flared to life to prove my point.

Jenny bowed her head to me. "I understand. I will convey your wishes to Tennyson."

"I'll tell him myself."

"As you wish."

I stood up to pace the room, knowing she wasn't done. I reined in my power to keep from losing it. How dare they doubt Nestor? My grandfather! I tried telling myself that it was Tennyson's way to doubt first and have no regrets later, but when it came to my family, that was unacceptable. Even Finley and his new wife. Riley was family now, and I wouldn't have it.

"There is more," I said.

"Yes, about your mother," she said.

"Go ahead!" I waved my arm in the air, because why not now?

"We located her for only a short time, but we were unable to apprehend her."

"Apprehend?"

"She isn't working with Brockton, but she has a side business that she ran under your father's nose. She is the one that heads up the fairy trafficking business. Of course, her business is down, because Oberon is no longer in charge. She's been on the run since we started looking for her. The remainder of the Sanhedrin are looking for her, as well. If they find her before we do, they will execute her."

"Trafficking fairies? Really?"

"We are totally sure on this. We wanted to be sure before we gave you the information. And considering your last threat about your family, I figured you should know everything."

"What is everything?"

"We believe that she was helping Demetris Lysander."

"Fuck. This is a nightmare," I said, sitting back down on the couch. I buried my head in my hands. I'd never been close to my mother, but I'd seen her in the Otherworld when Brockton tried to kill me with a nail gun. She had come on to Dylan just to test him.

"This causes problems for you because of relation. She is your mother. She is Nestor's daughter. When the fairies here find out, there might be backlash. We would like to keep it on the downlow until after the battle. That way…"

"No. We will tell them. If they don't want to fight with me, then that is their choice. I have had nothing to do with my mother's crimes, nor has Nestor. I suppose you questioned him about that as well."

"We did. He knew nothing."

"Of course he didn't!"

"I know you are angry."

"Really? What was your first clue, Jenny? Are you enjoying roasting my mother who gave Arthur the heir he needed?" It was a low blow, but I was pissed.

"What's wrong?" Levi's voice echoed through my head.

"Not now."

"Grace."

"Ask Tennyson. He knows."

I felt his presence back-off. Bless him. He knew when to push my buttons, and he knew when to leave well enough alone.

"Mother was helping Lysander build an army for Brockton."

"We think that she didn't know the connection, because once your father killed Lysander, your mother's actions changed. We were able to trace back some of her activities. After we take back Winter, Tennyson wants to start a task force of our people to go and help some of these fairies that have been sold off to the highest bidder. Your mother has made a lot of money from it, and currently avoids our detection because of it."

"Is she tied up with Kyffin Merrick, too?"

"We have not made a solid connection, yet."

"That's why you are searching for him. To see if he is connected to my mother's activities. When did you start suspecting her?"

"When Brockton shot those nails into your leg, he had you on camera. A fairy auction. He had no intentions of selling you, but he wanted the whole underbelly of the fairy world to see that he had killed you, making him powerful enough to take the throne from your father. Troy and his men confiscated the equipment that Brockton used to film you, and that evidence disappeared from police custody."

"Tennyson took it."

"One of his men, actually. He was able to verify that the equipment came from a company tied to Niles Babineau. Niles also submitted to the moonshine test. It is why he is here now. He did not know that your mother was using one of his companies to run her trade. We think that when she saw the video of you, she cut all ties with Babineau, Merrick, and ceased the trafficking until after your father's death. She escaped the siege of the Otherworld and did what she could here to keep herself hidden from us and you. Tennyson saw you that day on the video and decided that if you lived, he would finally do what your father asked of him."

"Which was?"

"Before you came to Shady Grove, your father asked Tennyson to watch after you. He tracked you down when you were with Remington. He tried to fix that problem by making a deal with Remington's wife. Phoebe was Rowan, Robin's mother. In the first life, she was Elaine who loved Tennyson and bore him Galahad. He offered himself to her if she would divorce Remington, so that you could be together.

The deal came too late, and you were too stubborn. Plus, Jeremiah moved you, per your father's request to Shady Grove, where he sent you a phoenix and a bard."

"Was Tennyson Robin's father?" I asked. Jenny winced, and I knew the truth. "I killed his daughter."

"Robin was never anything but a vessel for Titania. Rowan never wanted a crown. She was too busy being a witch here. Rhiannon didn't like that she'd chosen that path over royalty, but Rhiannon capitalized on her pregnancy to place Titania as the daughter of the great knight Lancelot. She immediately took the child from Rowan. Tennyson knew when Robin was born that she was never his daughter. She was just a shell for more of Rhiannon's plans and machinations. Morgana always wanted Lancelot, but he hated her. Elaine only had him because she used a trick to look like me. Witches. Anyway, he is not angry with you. This was all part of Rhiannon's way of getting back at Tennyson for rejecting her so many times."

"No wonder you didn't want anything to do with him. You didn't know why he was with Elaine again. Did you?"

"I didn't, but it turns out that no matter how much I tried to hate him, I still loved everything about us."

"How can I be Queen when I am so blind to all of this? Just when I think I've got a handle on it, something else happens. Truth happens and it slaps me in the face."

"It jerks a knot in your tail."

My gaze met hers, and I saw the humor, but I also saw the loyalty and love of a friend.

"I'm so sorry."

She moved across the couch and hugged me.

"You are the Queen we need. Let us handle the dirty work. We are good at it. Just trust us to do what is right by you. I swear that we always will."

"The two of you are a force to be reckoned with, for sure." I pulled away from the hug.

"So are you and the bard."

"The King."

47

She laughed. "Yes, the little bard King."

"He's not little at all," I replied.

"Oh really?"

"Really."

We switched to wine. Talked about men and sex. One last night to just be Grace Ann Bryant with her friend Jenny from the block. Rufus quietly watched us giggle and laugh like silly girls. Until he curled up at my feet to sleep.

CHAPTER SEVEN

I DIDN'T SLEEP. AT ALL. JENNY SLEPT ON THE COUCH PEACEFULLY. I paced the house, going over all the things she'd told me about my mother and the sacrifice that Tennyson had made for me, which eventually resulted in me killing his daughter.

Rufus followed close behind me wherever I walked. Occasionally, he would nudge my leg to remind me that he was still there.

Something didn't add up. It seemed as though this all worked out in the end, but how much of the beginning was orchestrated? Did Rhiannon somehow put Remington in my life so that I would like him? Maybe so she could manipulate Phoebe/Rowan to leave him for Tennyson, opening the door for a child to be the vessel for an ancient ruler? Who was also the beginning of the end for Dylan. My head spun with the what ifs.

"Grace." Levi. Of course, he could feel my anxiety.

"Hey."

"You okay?"

"Can't sleep. Did he tell you?"

"Yeah."

"I feel stupid."

"You have never been stupid. I've known you to pretend to not pay attention on purpose or pretend to be stupid. But you are smart and have made all the right choices since you became Queen of the Exiles."

"You are biased."

"You deserve to have a biased partner in your corner."

"I'm not sure I deserve any of this."

"Shut up."

"What?!"

"You heard me. I said, shut up."

"Levi middle name I can't say Rearden."

He chuckled in my head. *"I'm not afraid of you, Gloriana. I stand behind you one hundred percent. I always will."*

"Just stand beside me."

"I'll do that too."

"See you later?"

"Wouldn't miss it for the world."

I felt the connection fade off, but the light touch of a tingle started at my neck, then radiated to my toes. That was a neat trick. It felt like he was right here. I closed my eyes and waited until the feeling faded.

However, I didn't rest. My mother needed to be found. Fairy trafficking was a heinous business. Fairies would be bound with magic and sold to the highest bidder. Most of the time they were sold to other, more powerful fairies, but there were instances that the influential and rich humans of the world would obtain a fairy slave. My stomach churned thinking about it. Why would my mother do such a thing? We weren't close, but I never suspected her of anything as terrible as this.

Just before dawn, Callum showed up at the house. He came through the back door and didn't expect to find me standing in the kitchen.

"Mom? You okay?" he asked.

"Hey. What are you doing here? I thought all of y'all were out at Tennyson's cabin?"

"I was, but I had an early patrol with the wolves today. I came home to get a shower and grab a few things for later. Haven't you slept?"

"No. A lot on my mind."

"I've been wanting to talk to you about the day that you killed Robin. We haven't had time."

"It was just a couple of days ago."

"I know. You've been busy with wedding plans."

"I know you made a choice that day, and I cannot thank you enough for making it."

"Watching him there, helpless, it about killed me. He stood up for me against Atohi, and I felt like I was letting him down. But, I knew he'd want me to save Winnie."

"You see, some people think that you saved Winnie for me, but I know you did it for him."

"I can move to Troy's place. I talked to him about it, and he said it was fine."

"Why would you move?"

"Aydan has a lot of learning and growing to do. Levi talked to me about it, and I already knew, but hearing him say it really sank in. It doesn't matter what I feel for him. He's not to that point in his life." The torn look on his tortured face made my mother's heart ache.

"If you leave now, it might hurt him."

"It will hurt us both."

"It will make three of us hurt," I added.

"Mom."

"I mean it. I know you will protect them like a big brother should."

"I can't be his brother."

"For now, you can."

"What will people say?"

"Nothing, and if they do, they are idiots." I touched his face. Callum had always had a serious maturity about his look. So young, but an old soul. "Everyone in this town knows that you're not biologically related. If at some point in the future, Aydan decides that he feels the same way about you, then not a soul in this town will say anything. I dare them, but you are right. For now, you are his brother. He needs you; Winnie needs you, and I need you. You are a blessing that I never saw coming. But one day, after you've given up the things that you want because of timing or because I'm awfully persuasive, you will get what you want. What you want between now and then might change, but your sacrifice and your giving heart will be rewarded."

"Good things don't always happen to good people."

"Sometimes you've got to have a little faith that everything will work out."

"Faith in what?"

"Family. Love."

He threw his arms around me and hugged me tight. "I've never felt so loved as I do here."

"That's because you are home, Callum." I continued to hold him, because he needed it. Perhaps I needed it too. I realized that I needed to have the same faith. Faith in my family and in love. That's what this whole day was to be about for all of the exiles. "Now, go get a shower. You stink like a sweaty dog."

He laughed releasing our embrace. "Well, I kinda am."

"Get," I said, shooing him away.

He ran off down the hallway to his room. When I turned to the living room, Jenny's eyes were open, but she hadn't moved from her spot on the couch.

"You are a damn fine mom, Grace," she said.

"Who would have thought?"

"Not me, but you are."

"I'm trying. It's not like there is a guidebook for parenting."

"Actually, there are quite a few, but you are doing fine without them. You follow your heart which is not a typical fairy trait."

"I dunno. Levi seems to have it down."

"It's just a coincidence that he has a piece of your heart inside of him, too."

"No. I'm pretty sure he'd be that way without me mucking it up."

"Maybe. Did you sleep?"

"No."

"You should have. It's your big day. The others will be arriving soon. At least, go upstairs, take a warm bath, and relax for an hour or so before the commotion starts," she suggested.

A warm bath did sound wonderful. Might as well go ahead and start my last day as Grace Ann Bryant. Even though Levi and I hadn't talked about names, it was the human tradition for the bride to take the grooms name. Grace Ann Bryant-Rearden didn't have the right ring to it. I contemplated the name thing while I walked up the steps. Winnie went whizzing by me.

"Morning, Mom."

"Morning."

"I'm going to make cereal."

"Alright. Jenny is down there, and Callum is in his bathroom."

"Okie-dokie. I will be a good host while you go upstairs."

"That's my girl."

I continued up while she ran off to the kitchen. Grace Ann Rearden didn't sound right either. Of course, since the importance of the wedding affected the Otherworld and fairies as a whole, we were simply Gloriana and Levi getting married. Levi, since he was raised in a human home, didn't have a fairy name. Except for his middle name, which neither one of us could speak. However, Matthew Rayburn could. As a druid, he could speak Levi's full name at the wedding. It was one of the reasons why I wanted Matthew to do the ceremony.

My mind wandered as the warm water ran into the tub. I chucked in one of the fizzy bombs that Levi had bought for me. I watched it twirl spreading purple, pink, and blue bubbles around the tub. While it started, I took off the clothes that I had worn all night and rolled my shoulders at the freedom in being naked. Dipping my toe in first, I tested the water as the flowery scent of the bomb filled the room.

Heaven couldn't describe how great it felt to slip into the pastel colored warm water and relax. All the tension of the night before soaked away. I looked through my sight, and I could see the slight shimmer of a spell. Levi had cast a relaxation spell on the bomb.

"Clever devil." Rufus stood beside the tub wagging his tail. "I didn't mean you."

Closing my eyes, I drifted off into the familiar touch of Levi's magic and a warm bath.

CHAPTER EIGHT

When I opened my eyes, two bright brown ones stared back at me.

"Can I put my dress on now, Momma?" Winnie asked.

"Not yet. Is everyone here?" I asked.

"All the girls are here. Aunt Jenny said the boys are staying with Uncle Tennyson."

"You've got all kinds of aunts and uncles now, don't you?" I asked.

"What can I say? I'm fabulous."

This child. "You certainly are."

"I want to see your dress. You are going to look beautiful."

"Thank you, Pumpkin." She handed me a towel, and I knew my bath was over. I climbed out and toweled off while she chatted about the flowers that Chaz and Ella had brought. Apparently, Betty and Luther had also arrived with snacks and a "ginormous" cake. When I stepped into the bedroom, a white robe hung from one of the posts on the bed. On the left breast, the word "Bride" had been embroidered in turquoise. I slipped into the plush robe and for just a moment, I allowed myself to feel like a queen.

I followed Winnie down into the main floor of the house. People were rushing around while Betty was giving orders. I stood in awe of the flowers and decorations that Chaz and Ella were sorting through. Every flat surface including the dining room table was covered in glass cylinders with ivory candles inside.

"See!" Winnie said.

"Wow," I muttered.

"Grace!" Ella exclaimed. She ran up and hugged me with her bulging belly. I felt the two little fairies inside through my connection to her.

"Soon," I said, looking at her.

"Gosh! I hope so," she grinned. "I'm about to pop!"

"No, it will be soon," I said.

"How do you know that?" she asked.

"I dunno." I wasn't sure, but it was a definite impression that I got from the two beings inside of her. All we needed was Ella going into labor during the ceremony.

Jenny calmly ordered people about the room, and I stood feeling helpless. Chaz informed me that he would do my hair first, then I'd get into my dress, but since we were waiting on twilight to have the ceremony, we still had all day. You would have thought the wedding was in five minutes the way everyone rushed around the room.

I sat down on a stool in the kitchen and sipped a cup of coffee when Callum emerged from his room.

"Hey, I didn't know you were still here," I said.

He leaned over and kissed my cheek. "I'm heading back over to Troy's house. I just needed a night to clear my head."

"See you this evening?" I asked.

"Of course. Love you, Mom," he said as he headed toward the garage. A few minutes later, I heard Dylan's old Camaro rumble to life. Callum left, and Nestor arrived.

He walked into the kitchen with a big grin on his face.

"We need to talk," I said sternly.

"About?" he asked.

"Frist."

"Grace, I'm old enough to make my own decisions about things.

This doesn't have anything to do with you. I passed all of Tennyson's tests," he said.

"Why?" I whispered.

"Cause sometimes even an old fella like me needs a little comfort," he replied.

"And she does that for you?" I asked.

"Yeah, she does."

I sighed. "You are right. It's none of my business."

"You wouldn't be my Grace if you didn't stick your nose somewhere it doesn't belong," he said with a slight chuckle. "I promise you, Gracie. I will never do anything on purpose to harm you."

I hugged him tightly. "I love you, Grandfather."

"I love you, too. Your brother tells me that he's giving you away," he said.

"I haven't talked to him, but that's what Riley said."

"I will do what you want. Your bond with your brother is important going forward. The forces in Winter respect him. Once you get there, you will need his full support."

"This isn't a political thing. This is a family thing."

"I get that, but I'm telling you that outwardly, your connection to him could be improved. This is a way to do that," Nestor explained.

"Do you know about Mom?" I asked.

"I know what they told me," he said. "It's hard to believe, but it could be true. Your mother wasn't the best person in the world. I loved her, because she was my daughter. Who knows what living in the Otherworld did to her or why she got involved with this? She isn't a part of this though." He pointed to me then back to himself.

"I don't understand it all," I said.

"Focus on one thing at a time. Today is your wedding day. No more of this talk," he said. "I suspect that is why Jenny told you last night. She didn't want to taint today and how special it is."

A marriage between a King and Queen was a special occasion, but inside, I fought all the things that plagued me about Jenny's talk and the upcoming war with Brockton. Brushing it all aside was easier said than done.

Bramble and Briar flew up to Jenny who ordered them outside to get the fairy guard to set a perimeter on the stone circle. She also emphasized that there would be no sex or role playing today. Briar rolled her eyes, and Bramble grumbled, but they both agreed, then whizzed out the front door which was being held open by a woman I didn't recognize.

I stood up pulling power to myself.

"Who the fuck are you?" I asked.

The tan-skinned woman stood in the doorway with a dagger in one hand and a basket in the other. She wore tight jeans and a sleeveless tank with a plunging neckline. I was pretty sure the back of the shirt didn't exist, but I couldn't tell for sure.

The room got very quiet except for Nestor who rushed to grab Winnie.

"Catrina!" Jenny exclaimed. "What are you doing here?"

"I have a delivery for Mr. Tennyson," she replied, as her eyes scanned the room. She was beautiful, but clearly deadly.

"How did you walk into my house past the wards?" I asked.

"Grace, she's one of ours," Jenny explained.

"I get that, but I still want an answer," I said.

The young woman sat down the basket, then turned her bare back to me. A bright tattoo exploded with light, covering her back from her neck to the waist of her jeans. The glowing skull had menacing teeth and flowery details. I knew what she was, but I had heard that all of La Calavera had died.

My tattoo still glowed with power. I looked down at it, then at hers and realized that there was some sort of commonality there. My tattoo didn't allow me to go through wards though. I looked through my sight at her and gasped.

"She's human."

"Yes, but don't let that fool you. That's enough, Catrina. You can stow the neon," Jenny said. The tattoo on her back faded and the woman turned back to us with the same deadly eyes. They were a dark brown, and I suspected her hair was dark brown naturally, but she had it dyed to make it lighter. Almost an orangey-brown color. It was piled neatly on her head in a tight bun with wisps of hair flowing around her face.

"I should have knocked, but the door was open," she said. It wasn't an explanation, as much as it was a condemnation of the lack of security.

"Grace Ann Bryant, please meet Catrina Morales," Jenny said, formally introducing the woman. I didn't budge to greet her.

"You are La Calavera. You hunt our kind and kill them," I said.

Her eyes hardened, and she took a deep breath before speaking. "La Calavera is dead. I killed them. All of them. I work for Tennyson Schuyler. He pays well."

Pulling power from my tattoo, the temperature in the room dropped, and the woman gripped her dagger tighter. My hair lost all color, turning to a brilliant white. My skin erupted in glowing swirls of Winter power. The woman took a step back, but only to move into a fighting stance.

"I am Gloriana, Queen of the Exiles, Heir to the Winter Throne, and I dust anyone that threatens my family." My voice sounded hollow as snow began to fall inside the living room. The woman slacked her stance and slowly placed her dagger on the ground.

"I am no threat to you," she said, holding her empty palms outward to me.

A swirling portal appeared in the dining room, and Tennyson and Levi stepped through with swords in hand. Tennyson put his away, but Levi held Excalibur ready to fight. He stepped slowly over to me but didn't speak.

"Catrina, it is good to see you. I hope you have something for me," Tennyson said.

"I do, Sir, but I seem to have pissed off the Snow Queen over there," she said without taking her eyes off me.

"Don't worry. That's not hard to do. Catrina works for me, Grace, and she is a very valuable employee. I do hope that you will not dust her," Tennyson said lightly.

"Dust me?" Catrina asked. "Look, Grace. Gloriana. Whatever your name is. I didn't mean any harm. I was looking for Tennyson, and someone said he was here. The door was open. I should have knocked."

"*I think we can probably stand down,*" Levi suggested.

"*I think I dust anyone who walks into my home carrying a weapon,*" I said.

"*Then why is she still standing there?*" Levi asked.

"*Shut up,*" I replied, releasing the power. Then I reached over and shoved him. The tension released in the room, and everyone laughed at Levi stumbling. He righted himself, then shook his head.

"He is not supposed to be here," Jenny fussed.

"Like I could make him stay behind when something was going on here," Tennyson replied.

Levi eyed the robe. Specifically, the part where it split open at my chest. I tucked it covering myself, and he sighed.

"Good morning, my Bride," he said.

"She is right. You aren't supposed to be here."

"I had to come rescue you."

"Since when did I need rescuing?"

"Don't make me answer that in front of everyone. I'd hate to undermine your authority."

"Get out of here!"

He grinned, then bowed. "My Queen." He twirled Excalibur opening a portal back to Tennyson's home and stepped through.

"That man," I grumbled. Winnie ran over to me and grabbed my hand. Her warmth coursed through me reminding me of Dylan's way of calming me after a Winter flare-up.

"I do apologize," Catrina said, drawing my attention back to her.

"Perhaps we should step outside, Grace. I suspect that this involves you," Tennyson said, looking down at Winnie. Whatever information Catrina had brought in her basket didn't need to involve Winnie or anyone else in the room.

"Sure. I'll be right back, Winnie. Go brush your hair so Chaz can fix it for you. Okay?" I said, looking up at Chaz.

He held his hand out to Winnie. "Come with me, Princess. Let's make you look fabulous!"

60

"Alright," Winnie said enthusiastically as Chaz, lead her away.

I straightened my robe and followed Catrina, Tennyson, and Jenny out onto the front porch.

"We need a little privacy, Grace," Tennyson said.

I wasn't really a spell kind of caster. My magic manifested differently because of its intrinsic nature. However, Levi had taught me a few things about spells, plus I remembered some of the things I'd been taught as a child. Pulling power from my tattoo, I spoke one word.

"Silence."

A bubble of privacy formed around us, shutting out the sounds of the bustling in the house, as well as, the breeze and birdsong from the outside.

"Thank you," Tennyson said. "Catrina, have you found your mark?"

"I always find my mark," she replied. She didn't seem to have much respect for any sort of authority except for when she realized she was dealing with me. She opened the basket to reveal the bulging eyed head of a man. "May I present, Kyffin Merrick."

"Yuck," I said.

"Where did you find him?" Tennyson asked.

"In Chinatown," she replied.

"Which Chinatown?" Tennyson asked.

"San Francisco," she replied.

"Did he tell you anything before you removed his head?" Tennyson asked.

"He was rather resistant to my methods, but I did not remove his head. A man in a mask jumped in the middle of our conversation and removed it in front of me. I had to make a choice. Bring you the head or chase the man."

"And you brought me the head."

"No, I chased the man. I lost him, but when I returned the head was waiting for me. The authorities hadn't found it. The body was removed by your cleaners," Catrina explained.

"Why was he in San Francisco? Was my mother there?" I asked.

She turned to me, then back to Tennyson.

"She outranks me. I suggest you answer her," Tennyson said.

"He was not with Ellessa. She goes by the name Lessa Arthur now. He last saw her in New Orleans, but I also know she has been in Las Vegas recently. She heard that you and Gloriana were there with the frog," Catrina said. "I will continue to hunt for her."

"Was he involved with the trafficking?" I asked, looking into the dead eyes of Kyffin Merrick.

"I do not know," Catrina said. "He was working with the one you call Sergio Krykos."

"Brockton," I said.

"Mordred," Tennyson added.

"Another law office in California was doing the same recruiting that they were doing here. It was why he was in San Francisco. I saw him open a portal through a tree and send creatures through it."

"If they were doing it in California, they could have been doing it anywhere," I gasped. "Instead of thousands of Wild Fairies, there could be hundreds of thousands."

"I sincerely doubt that Brockton has the gifts necessary to keep that many Wild Fairies in check. Grace, we will check it thoroughly before we make a move on Winter. Finley has requested that he be allowed to go in before us. He knows the layout better than anyone else here, and he will be able to come back with the information that we need," Tennyson said.

I didn't want Finley going into Winter alone. I knew that he was our best bet as a spy, but the thought of losing him now hurt. He had volunteered, and I knew there was little that I could do outside of ordering him to stay. "We will talk about it later," I said.

"Is there anything else, Catrina?" Tennyson asked.

"No, Sir."

"You are welcome to stay for the wedding," I offered.

"I'm not a wedding kind of girl," she replied.

"She will stay because I need to talk to her more about all of this," Tennyson said.

"But..." Catrina started to protest, but she quickly squashed it. Tennyson had something on her. I wasn't sure what it was, but a person could only be manipulated so far before they would turn on you. For me, it made her a liability. Someone to be watched very closely.

"Good. I thought you would see it my way. Sorry for the interruption, Grace. Go back to your wedding preparations," he said.

Jenny, who had been totally silent through the whole conversation, snaked her arm through mine and guided me back into the house. Once the door shut, I had to ask.

"What is he holding over her?"

"It's not like that. He's actually helping her. She's very good at what she does, but she got herself in a mess. Tennyson is helping her get out of it. In exchange, she works for him," she said. "Nothing to worry about. At her core, Catrina is a good person, if somewhat misguided occasionally."

"She needs to not be misguided in my presence."

"Noted," Jenny replied. "Now. You sit down over here on the couch. Relax and drink some coffee. Chaz will be finished with Winnie soon, then he will work on you."

"Is there nothing I can do to help?" I asked.

"Nope." She marched off to the dining room to help Ella and Betty sort the flowers. Nestor had disappeared, but I figured he was pretty close by. Before long, Wendy and Riley arrived along with Finley. He and I talked about Catrina's appearance and his decision to go into Winter. There was no convincing him otherwise.

"You need me there, Grace. I'm the one that has to go."

I knew he was right, but my heart tugged at that familial bond. My brother. Practically my twin. "I know," I replied simply.

He kissed my forehead. "I've let you down before. I swear to you that I won't this time. We will take back our father's throne, and you will sit upon it as you have always deserved."

"Fin, did you know your mother?" I asked.

"Not really. I was raised by some of Father's knights. Her name was Ashryn, and she, like your mother, was part of Father's harem. She died after you were banished from the Otherworld. Father had a funeral for her as he did for most of his wives. I was there, but I didn't know her," he said.

"Were you sad?" I asked.

"Yes, but probably not as much as I should have been. I was a dick in those years. Nothing I did made Father happy, and I spent most of my time above the surface keeping an eye on you," he said.

"You could have told me you were there," I suggested.

"I should have. Looking back, I wanted two different things. One of those things was to please Father. He presented me as an heir to the entire kingdom. It was a title I didn't want. I still don't want it. I'm relieved that you are marrying Levi that way no one gets any ideas about King Finley," he said.

"I'd follow King Finley." He smiled and shook his head. "What was the other thing you wanted?"

"To be free of it all. I saw you up here living your life as you pleased. You were on the run from the Sanhedrin, but you were not bound by any laws or expectations."

"Everything is laws and expectations now." I sighed thinking about all my responsibilities.

"Yes, but you handle it well. I don't see you running anymore," he said with a smile.

"I'm not running. The people in this room are my life. That man waiting to marry me means everything to me. My boys. The wolves. Every fairy alive is watching this today, and I feel it. I need you here, so don't go off into the Otherworld and do something stupid. You have a wife to consider now," I said.

"And a child," he added.

"What!? Finley!"

"Yeah," he replied, looking across the room to Riley. Her eyes lifted from the table covered with flowers and put her hands on her hips. She shook her head.

"You just couldn't wait to tell her!" she protested.

I rushed across the room and hugged her. When I pulled back to look at her, she seemed shocked. "I gotta love any woman that can make an honest man out of my brother," I said.

"He wanted to tell you. I'm sorry I didn't tell you last night," she said.

I reached for her belly, and she nodded when I hesitated to get permission. Her belly showed no signs of pregnancy, but when my hand rested on it, I could feel the life inside it. A quickly pumping heartbeat resonated through my veins. The next generation of Bryants'.

"If you say it's twins, I'm going to die," Finley quipped.

"It's just one. A strong steady heartbeat," I said.

"We were going to tell you after the wedding, but *someone* couldn't wait," Riley scolded him. He hugged her, then kissed her temple.

"I'm sorry. I'm excited," he replied.

The room erupted in congratulations. Jenny ran to the kitchen to grab the pitcher of sweet tea. She went around the room refilling everyone's glass, then lifted hers, "To the next generation of royalty!"

"Cheers!" Ella said.

Chaz entered the room with Winnie whose hair was twisted and curled. She looked like a proper princess. "We are toasting that Winnie is going to have a new cousin soon," I informed them.

Chaz covered his mouth with surprise, and Winnie ran up to us. "Can I touch?"

Riley giggled, then nodded. Winnie placed her hand on Riley's flat stomach. "Gosh, her hands are warm."

"Phoenix," I said.

"Was *he* like this?" Riley asked.

"Yeah," I replied.

"Wow!"

"I don't feel nuthin'," Winnie said.

"Anything," I corrected.

"Nuthin'," she repeated. "Not a thing."

"That's because it's still early on. Once the baby grows inside of her, you will be able to feel it kick." Looking at Riley, I said, "You should stay away from the fighting."

"No, you will need the witches," she protested.

"I won't risk your child's life," I said.

"Grace, you traipsed across summer when you were pregnant with Aydan. You were fine. I'll be fine, too," she argued.

"Finley, talk some sense into her," I pleaded.

"We will keep her and the child safe," he said with confidence. I didn't like the risk, but now wasn't the time to talk about it. Levi and I could discuss it later, and maybe both of us could make them see that it wasn't wise to stick a pregnant woman in the middle of a war. My gaze drifted to Ella who was about to pop. There was no way in this world that Astor would let her be involved with the siege on the Otherworld. I planned on making sure my brother saw the error of his ways.

"Where is Kady?" I asked. I seemed to be asking that a lot lately.

"I haven't heard from her today. I'll call Wendy and see if they are on their way," Riley said, fishing a cell phone out of her pocket.

"Flipping the subject won't change my opinion, Glory. I know how you operate," Finley scolded me.

"You don't have a clue as to how I can operate if needed," I warned him.

"Riley and I will make the decision together when the time comes. We may not have to worry about it. We may not need the witches," he reasoned.

"Damn it, Fin. That is your child," I said.

"I understand that. The decision isn't made yet, but we will make it. Not you or Levi."

Everyone else in the room shied away from the conversation by keeping up their own chats even though we both knew they were listening to us.

Finley was right. He and Riley had the final say on what they would do, but I hoped to the goddess that they would choose to protect that child. My niece. I didn't tell them the gender because Levi had scolded me before when I started to tell Ella what she was having. I'd turned into a supernatural ultrasound machine. We didn't need no stinking doctors here.

Which made me think of Tabitha and Stephanie. Their reappearance threw me off, and even though I wanted to be mad at Levi, I couldn't be. Not because it was our wedding day, but because I knew how manipulative Lilith could be. I recalled the moments where I'd used all of my power in the Battle of Trailer Swamp. My conscious-ness had drifted to her in the Tree of Life. She'd used Dylan's image to tempt me, even though I knew Dylan wasn't there.

My attention was drawn to the door as Amanda arrived with Mark who wore a smart little tuxedo. Levi had chosen him as our ring bearer. Soraya was with them. I wasn't sure why she hadn't come with Luther and Betty, but I didn't ask. She was dressed in a bright yellow gown which made her caramel colored skin radiant. She was a pretty little girl with her dark black hair and piercing blue eyes.

"Well, Mark, don't you look handsome," I said. "And Miss Soraya, you look lovely." Soraya smiled, then curtseyed.

"Thank you, ma'am," Mark said very properly. His eyes darted around the room, and I knew he was looking for a certain little girl. Almost on cue, Winnie descended the stairs in her flower girl dress which was a cobalt blue with silver accents. The tulle skirt belled out around her legs and glittered in the sunlight. Mark's gaze fixed on her, and the poor kid's mouth dropped open. They were too young for this shit, but there it was. Amanda looked at me, and her brow furrowed. I tilted my head sideways questioning her, but she shook her head in response. Mark had hardly paid attention to Winnie when they played yesterday, and it had bothered her. Now, however, the little future alpha wolf seemed to be tuned in to my phoenix daughter.

"Hello, Mark," Winnie said politely as she passed him without a second look. I pressed my lips together when the disappointment registered on Mark's face. "Momma, how do I look?" Winnie twirled in place.

"You look gorgeous," I replied.

Mark walked up next to her. "You look very pretty, Winnie."

"Thank you, Mark. Raya, let's go up to my room and play," Winnie said. Soraya nodded, and the two girls ran up the stairs leaving poor Mark alone. I needed to talk to Winnie about excluding her friends, but now wasn't the time.

"Mark, why don't you go in the kitchen and help Luther? I'm sure he can find something for you to do," I said.

"Yeah, come on, Mark. I got something for ya," Luther called out.

Mark hung his head, stuck his hands in his pockets, and sauntered into the kitchen.

"What was that?" I asked Amanda once he got into the kitchen.

"He can still hear us," she said.

"Well?"

She pressed her lips together and reluctantly spoke. "He talked about her from the moment she left yesterday until we got here this morning."

"Winnie said he didn't play with her at all."

"He didn't. He's afraid of her."

"Afraid? Did she do something to him?" Winnie's temper had gotten much better, but I didn't know what had happened at their house yesterday.

"No, nothing like that. He's chosen her," she said.

I shook my head. "Nope. They are too young for that."

"Grace, you have no control over it, and neither do I. Winnie may not choose him, but his desires won't change. For now, it's a need to protect her no matter what. Which he always has, but it's more now. He would give his life for her, even at this young age."

"She's not wolf," I said.

"Doesn't matter. The protection instinct will grow over the years as they age, and eventually, he will love her. From my experience, an early imprint like this is a deep one. If she doesn't choose him, it will scar him for life. He knows that and he also knows how strong-willed and free spirited she is."

"And so he's afraid that one day she won't feel the same about him," I concluded.

"Yeah. I'm sorry, but there isn't anything we can do to change his mind," she said.

"How did this happen all of a sudden?"

"I don't think it did. It's always been there. He just finally decided to accept it."

I looked into the kitchen where Luther had put Mark to work. Through my sight, I saw the handsome young man that he would become. I knew Winnie could see that in him, too. I had no idea what that meant for their futures, but I knew my girl. She wouldn't give in to him easily, if ever. Mark had matured a lot since his alpha senses had emerged. Winnie hadn't seemed to reach that point. They were only seven years old, but in the world of fairies and weres, kids matured faster than normal. Not just the rapid aging of fairy babies, but in general, this life had a way of pushing you to adulthood much faster than any parent could ever want.

When I first saw Winnie as a tiny baby, I loved her instantly. She wasn't mine back then, but something in my heart told me that she was. I wanted to hold on to those moments because I had lost them with Aydan. My experiences around the human world had changed my perspective from the norm of fairy childrearing. I wondered how Ella and Astor would raise their kids, and Riley and my brother. Would they let their children age rapidly or hold on to those innocent years? Another decision that I couldn't make for them. I hadn't had a choice with Aydan, but I did with Winnie. It felt right to allow her to age at her own pace instead of accelerating her growth.

"Will he age quicker?" I asked Amanda.

"No, but he will mature faster than most kids his age."

"I already see that in him. It will take a while for her to catch up to him."

"I know wolves, and I know alphas. He will wait for her."

"I hope he's got more patience than I do."

"Me too," Amanda said, nudging me with her elbow.

"I can crack on myself, but you are not allowed," I smirked.

"Oops," she replied. "Are you ready for today?"

"Not hardly, but I better get ready, because it's happening," I said.

"It's going to be a beautiful wedding and you need to enjoy every moment of it," Amanda said.

Nestor walked out of the kitchen with a cup of coffee. "Here, you look like you need this."

"Thanks. Amanda's son is already planning his wedding with my daughter," I huffed.

Amanda laughed, but Nestor looked alarmed. "He chose her?"

"He did," Amanda said.

"They are too young."

"I agree, but he has chosen her. I can see it in him. He won't ever want anyone else," Amanda explained.

"Even if she ends up with someone else?" I asked.

"I'm not sure. I've never seen an alpha not get their mate."

I snarled at the word mate. I didn't like the connotation.

"It's not like that, Grace," Nestor said. "I'm not happy about it either, but this is Mark we are talking about. They have been friends and will continue to be. They will have ups and downs, and who knows, maybe one day, they will fall in love."

"He's right. Mate is a one-sided term. It just means he chose her. She gets to accept it or not. And if she doesn't, it will be okay. He's going to be a strong leader one day with or without a partner," Amanda said with pride.

"I have no doubt of that," I said, looking down into Nestor's magical coffee. I took a long hot sip and pondered the future of my little wildfire.

CHAPTER NINE

"Grace, where is your dress?" Chaz asked.

"Hell, if I know? It was here yesterday," I said.

"Crap," he said, picking up his cell phone.

"Is it not here?!" I asked.

"I can't find it. Don't worry. We will find it," he coaxed.

Wendy burst through the door, and we stopped our activities.

"We have a problem," she said. Her face indicated it was much more than a lost dress.

"What is it?" I asked.

"Kady is gone," she said.

"Gone?" I asked.

"Caleb is..."

"No," I muttered. "She's gone to the ORCs. LEVI!"

A portal opened, and Levi rushed through in a navy suit with a white shirt. Tennyson was on his heels.

"What is it?!" he asked.

Wendy spoke, because none of the rest of us could. "Caleb is dead. Kady is gone."

"Matthew?" I asked.

"I didn't see any sign of him," Wendy said.

"I'll handle it. You stay here," Levi said sternly.

"I'm going with you," I said.

"In your Bride robe?" he asked.

I snapped my fingers, and my old glamour snapped into place. Brown hair, brown eyes, cut-off jeans and a tank top. "This will have to do," I said.

Levi took my hand, as Tennyson opened a new portal. We stepped through to the Rayburn house. No lights were on inside, but the front door was open. Reaching out with my senses, I could smell the dead body.

"Let us go inside, Grace," Levi said, squeezing my hand.

"I've seen dead bodies before," I said.

He touched my cheek and looked into my eyes. "This day should be a happy day. No need to fill it with bad memories."

"It's too late for that," I said.

"Come on," Tennyson said, holding his sword up. I pulled power which flowed from me to Levi. Our tattoos flared to life as we stepped into the quiet house. Searching through each room, we found nothing. The home had been rebuilt by one of Niles Babineau's crews after Robin burned it down. My heart pounded harder with each empty room.

"He's upstairs," I said.

Tennyson led the way while Levi followed me up. When we reached the room on the end of the hallway, we found Caleb Martin laying in the bed. Tennyson didn't pay attention to the body; he went to the bedside where an empty glass sat on the side table. He picked it up and took a sniff. Caleb seemed to be quietly sleeping.

"Poison?" Levi asked.

"Yes," Tennyson said finally looking at the body. He took the sheet and pulled it over his head. "If Matthew isn't here, we have to assume she took him with her."

"Or Mable is using Matthew to manipulate Kady," I said.

"Grace, Kady has never been totally in our camp," Levi said. "Surely you've felt it."

72

"I have, but I hoped that she was happy. Why kill Caleb? Why not just leave?" I asked.

"I don't know," Tennyson said. "It's a waste."

Levi pulled out his phone. After a quick dial, I heard Troy on the other line. Levi told him what we found. It only took about five minutes for Dominick and Troy to arrive.

"What do you want to do with his body?" Troy asked.

"He doesn't have any family here," I said.

"Kady was his everything," Dominick groaned.

"We were his family. We will have a funeral for him tomorrow. We can store the body in the old clinic," Levi said.

"Grace, you need to go home," Tennyson said.

"I'm not much in the wedding mood now," I said from my seat on the couch. Levi kneeled on the ground in front of me.

"We can't let anyone stop the wedding. That is what they want. We will do whatever you want to do, but before the night falls, you will be my wife," Levi said, caressing my neck with his hand.

"Do you think they did this just to stop us?"

"We can't rule it out," he replied.

A tear slipped down my cheek. Caleb was a casualty of a war we hadn't begun to fight. Our first move needed to be this wedding. "I'll go home."

"I'd kiss you, but I'm on restrictions," he said.

"What?! Jenny isn't here," I said.

"No, but I am," Tennyson said behind him.

"He's kept me away from you all day and all night," Levi grinned.

"Ridiculous," I muttered while Nick and Troy snickered.

Levi stood and helped me stand. "Stay focused. I'll see you later tonight," he said.

"The suit looks nice," I said.

"Just wait until you see the bow tie," he said with a wink.

"Bow ties are lame," Nick said.

"Shut it, Doggo," Levi teased. I managed a grin. "*It is taking every-thing I have not to kiss you right now, but I really don't want to piss off*

Tennyson which means pissing off Jenny. You have to admit the tentacles are scary."

"*Wimp. Come on, man up,*" I taunted him.

He closed his eyes and let out an internal groan. "Later."

"Promise?"

"Promise."

* * *

When I entered the house after Tennyson took me back, everyone seemed to be in the same places they were when I left.

"How bad was it?" Nestor asked.

"Looks like he went in his sleep," I said.

"Small mercies," Nestor said. He walked up and hugged me. "There was nothing you could have done."

"She's been acting strange lately," I said.

"We have to assume she is with the ORCs," Jenny said.

"Yes, but maybe she is being coerced since Matthew is gone too," I suggested.

"I doubt she took Matthew into Winter. Tennyson will have someone looking for him, and now we have to find a minister for the wedding," Jenny said.

"Shit. I didn't think about that. Levi says they did this to disrupt the wedding," I said.

"Nothing is stopping this wedding," Chaz said.

"Agreed! Which means you need to get your ass upstairs and let Chaz do your hair and make-up," Jenny said.

"Did you find my dress?" I asked. The look on her face told me everything. The dress was missing. "Fine. I'll wear whatever I conjure."

"We will find it!" I heard her call up to me as I climbed the stairs. Chaz followed me with a bag full of implements. It looked like torture to me.

"Since when do fairy queens need make-up?" I asked.

"This is all part of the experience, Grace. It's not about how pretty you are without make-up. It's a statement that you are putting your best face forward no matter what is thrown at you," Chaz explained as I took a seat in a chair he'd prepared in my bathroom.

"I think this is my best face," I said as I looked in the mirror. I realized I still had my glamour up. I dropped it. "I mean this one." *Your true self.*

"You are gorgeous. I'm just going to compliment it," he said laying out brushes and compacts all over the counter. "Don't scowl at my weapons. You fight your fight. I'll fight mine."

"We might need a lion in the fight," I said.

"You don't want me on a battlefield," he replied.

"You carried a sword at one time."

"How do you know that?"

"I can read."

"Damn books. You are starting to act like Levi. Reading books and shit."

I laughed at him. It wasn't meant as a compliment, but I saw it as one. "I'm not asking you to go, Chaz. I'm sure you have a purpose here."

"I'll have two little babies to watch over by then, and I'll do whatever else I can to help those who stay behind," he explained.

"That sounds perfect. Hair and make-up for everyone!"

"You tease, but sometimes a haircut and an open mind are all someone needs."

"You certainly helped me over the years."

"I'm glad to hear it. I'm also very pleased to see you happy again despite all the dark and gloomy going on, and if you ever get tired of Levi, send him my way."

"Hands off my man!"

He shrugged. "Can't blame a girl for trying."

I watched as he meticulously combed all of my platinum hair, then proceeded to put mounds of product in it in order to make it wavy just the way he wanted. There was something relaxing about a professional fixing your hair. I tried to sit back and forget that the war was getting more and more complicated by the moment. Instead, I ended up making a list of the difficulties. We were down a witch. They had gained one. They had the possibility of hundreds of thousands of wild fairies fighting on their side. My mother could possibly be in bed with the enemy or perhaps just a whole new enemy. Our direct link to the castle had moved to the fountain which put us days away from the center of Winter.

"You are beginning to brood like him too," Chaz warned. "Don't let it all get you down. I've seen you overcome every obstacle in your way. You will find your way through this one too. Gene and I have always known that you would be the one to come along and be the queen we needed. I admit when you showed up in your cut-off jean shorts and sassy, vulgar mouth, I wasn't so sure, but you've more than proved yourself."

I grabbed his hand as he applied something to my face. "Charles, thank you. That means more than you know."

He twisted his mouth. "You are welcome, but if you ever call me Charles again, I'll shave your head." I laughed with him and tried to let go of my burdens for the next few hours.

CHAPTER TEN

Winnie and Soraya slipped into the room as Chaz finished up my mascara. I was sure my eyelashes were now two inches long.

"You look beautiful, Miss Grace," Soraya said.

"Thank you, sweetheart. You look pretty cute yourself," I said. "Winnie, you need to get over whatever you are mad about and go play with Mark."

"Aw, Mom. He's stupid and weird," she groaned.

"Wynonna Riggs! Don't make me smack your butt in that dress. That was very rude. You can be sassy all you want, but you will not be rude. Do you understand?"

"Not really."

Chaz laughed, and I smacked him on the ass. "Damn, woman, you almost made me want to be straight."

"Winnie, you can be strong-willed and stubborn. Those are good traits to have sometimes. But I won't tolerate being mean or rude. Mark is your friend. He's going through a lot of changes in his life. You are too with all your fiery powers. It would be better for you to be understanding and kind."

"When do I get to be stubborn?"

"When he doesn't treat you right. Has he ever treated you badly?"

"No, ma'am. But he didn't play with me."

"Do you know why he didn't?"

"He said he needed to watch his sisters."

"That's right. He's very protective of them. He's protective of you, too."

"They are more important than me," she pouted. My heavens. It was jealousy rearing its ugly green head.

"For now, they are, but I promise you that one day, they won't be," I assured her.

"How do you know?"

"Because I'm the momma and I know everything!"

She hugged me. "I'm so glad you're my momma."

"I love being your momma." I hugged her back tightly. "Now, be mindful of your dress, but go find Mark."

"Yes, ma'am," she said, grabbing Soraya's hand racing out of the room.

"Good job, Mom. You are effectively teaching her to be just like you," Chaz quipped.

"And?" I replied, getting a good look at myself in the mirror. "Holy shit!"

"You like?"

"It looks great, Chaz."

"You're welcome," he said.

"Now if only I had a dress," I said.

"They will find it."

"I'm not counting on it. Maybe I should get married nude."

"I don't have enough foundation for that."

"Ah! You!"

He tilted his head and shrugged. "Well, I don't."

"Are you done with me?" I asked.

"Yes."

I kissed him on the cheek. "Thank you, Charles."

"Damn it, Grace!"

I laughed as I marched myself back downstairs where it had gotten pretty quiet. Jenny sat in my recliner dozing but perked up when she heard me on the steps.

"Well, Chaz works miracles."

I shook my head at her. "Where did everyone go?"

"Everyone is making their final preparations for the wedding. Winnie, Soraya, Mark, and the brownies are upstairs in her room. I had to convince them that today wasn't the day for outside play. Luther is setting things up in the back yard for the reception. Nestor is helping him, and I'm here waiting on you," she said.

"What's next?" I asked.

"I wanted you to know that although Tennyson and I love you very much, and technically I'm your step-mother of sorts, we will be standing in as Levi's parents tonight," she said.

My lip quivered and a tear threatened to fall. "I think that's wonderful."

"Good. Have you decided who is giving you away?" she asked.

"No. I think Nestor wants to do it, and I'm pretty sure that Finley wants to as well," I said.

Someone moved in the kitchen and for a moment, my breath caught in my chest. My son looked more like his father every day. Today, he reminded me of the night Dylan and I went to Amanda and Troy's wedding. He wore a black suit with a white shirt open at the neck. His sandy blond hair tossed the same way his father's did.

"I spoke to Finley and Nestor, and they both agreed that I should give you away," Aydan said. "I'll be representing Winnie and Callum."

He stood tall and confident. I couldn't speak for a moment looking at the young man standing before me.

"If you cry, you'll ruin your make-up," Jenny warned.

"Are you sure?" I asked him, fighting back the make-up ruination.

"Mom, of course I am. Besides I need one last reminder to that bard that he better take good care of you," he grinned.

"Your father would be so proud of you." I touched his cheek.

"Well, I haven't done much with myself, but I plan on making sure the Riggs name is carried properly," he said.

"I have no doubt that you will," I said. He lost the confidence for a moment, and I felt a question coming.

"What is it?"

"What's your name going to be after tonight?" he asked.

"Mom."

"Smartass," Jenny muttered behind me.

"Really though." Aydan definitely had more to say on the subject. I was interested in his wisdom on the matter. I'd seen flashes of the thunderbird inside of him, especially when Atohi was here. I knew he had it in him. He just needed the confidence to share that wisdom with the world. Might as well start with his mother.

"Levi and I haven't decided yet."

"It should be Rearden," Aydan said.

"Why do you say that?" I asked.

"When you were engaged to Dad, were you going to be a Riggs?" he asked.

"Yes," I replied.

"What makes Levi any different? It's not like Bryant is your real name. Levi's name is his and it's not made up," he said.

"Aydan, your name isn't made up," I said, thinking that's what he was thinking.

"No, Mom." I got the frustrated teenager look. "I was born with mine. It's mine. You can't go into the Otherworld or anywhere else with fairies and use the name, Grace Ann Bryant. Sure, they know the name, but Gloriana is who you are. Once you are married to Levi, Gloriana Rearden is who you are with him. A combined force. I know I've not been at this fairy stuff for very long, but that means something. You guys are doing this to be a combined entity. Using his name just adds to that statement. And for once, do something traditional."

I laughed hard at the last statement. "You don't know anything about me, Little Bird!"

"Actually, Levi and Troy have told me a lot of stories," he said.

"Oh! Have they? Looks like I've got some knots to jerk," I scowled.

"Nothing bad though. You've been through a lot of shit," he said.

"So, you want me to be a Rearden?" I asked to clarify.

"I want you to be happy, but yeah, it seems right to me."

"Honestly, it seems right to me too," I admitted.

"Now that that is settled, we need to decide on a minister," Jenny said. "I was thinking that we could grab Judge Chastain. Remy is an option, but that would probably be torture for him."

"Not Remy. He's suffered enough," I said.

"Niles is in town. I suppose he could do it," Jenny offered.

"One of our kind. I want a fairy," I responded.

A wide grin grew on Jenny's face. "I have an idea."

"I'm afraid," I replied.

She just laughed then stepped outside with her cell phone. I supposed that I didn't get to know her idea.

"I'm going back over to Tennyson's house to make sure Levi doesn't try to back out," Aydan said.

"Back out!"

He winked at me, then walked out the front door. I heard a *whomph* sound, then the flapping of large wings. I stepped outside to watch my son soar across the sky. He didn't shift very often, but when he did, it was breathtaking. Definitely not a little bird anymore.

Jenny said good-bye to whomever she was talking to on the phone and hung up. "It's taken care of now."

"Who is doing it?" I asked.

"It's a surprise," she replied.

"Okay," I said not wanting to fight. "And the dress?"

"Still working on that one. The spare dresses we had are gone too," she said.

"What the hell? Is someone just trying to annoy me? I'll just dress myself," I said.

"No, you won't. We will get a dress," she replied.

"Not that big cupcake thing," I protested.

She laughed but didn't comment. I'd wear my short silver dress before I wore that thing.

"Why don't you go inside and rest a little before the hullabaloo gets started?" she suggested.

"It's already started!" I protested.

"Just the tip of the iceberg," she said with a grin.

I stepped back inside, shaking my head once again at the whole ordeal. At least I hadn't had to do any of the planning myself, but now I was worried that I should have. When I sat on the couch, Rufus jumped up and curled himself in my lap. I brushed his fur and talked to him like I used to when it was just us.

"Rufus, you are a bad dog, but I love you." He nuzzled my hand, so I continued to pet. "What do you think of all this wedding stuff?" He began to wiggle his back leg as I found his favorite spot under his neck. "I just want it to be over and done, so we can get down to business." Rufus rolled over on his back so I could scratch around his chest. When I paused, he flapped his paws begging for more. "Rotten dog."

My mind drifted to Dylan and his dream. The original one where he and I would have gotten married in a perfect setting. I hoped it wasn't wrong to be thinking of him on the day I was to marry Levi. I didn't think Levi would be offended. He seemed to have a much better grasp on all of this than I did. Dylan would have married me immediately, but I wasn't ready. Was I ready now? I'd run from every relationship I'd ever had. Maybe that was what was unsettling me now. Maybe I wasn't as ready as I thought.

I closed my eyes and thought about the field where Dylan died. When I opened my eyes, I sat in the grass close to where we'd held the bonfire that night. The sun shined brightly above me, but its warmth didn't sink in to my skin. I felt cold in this place.

All my connections to Dylan were now my children and a book I hadn't read in my vault. Levi's story of what happened in the Otherworld. Maybe it was time that I did that, but today wasn't the day for it. Tomorrow was a war. I wasn't sure there would ever be time.

"I miss you," I said to the field. A warm breeze blew though the grass and tickled my skin. "Am I doing the right thing? I feel a little lost today and you always had a way of putting me back on track."

There was no answer. At least not one from Dylan.

I didn't hear him arrive, but I felt his presence. He settled in the grass behind me and wrapped his arms around me. Without saying a word, Levi answered my question.

After a few minutes of sitting in silence, he spoke. "I miss him, too."

"I just needed a moment to remember," I said.

"I'll call it all off. We will find a way to win this without the wedding. We will do whatever is best for you," Levi said.

"No, that's not why I am here," I protested. "Besides what is best for our children is to go through with this and put an end to the fighting."

"Even if we win Winter, there will always be a fight for what is right. It's why beings like Dylan and now Aydan exist. They fight for what is right. You've become one of those beings and I'm just privileged to join you in it."

"I couldn't do it without you."

"I think that is a lie." He chuckled softly.

"Fairies can't lie. Not about the important things."

He moved around to sit in front of me. His denim eyes darkened with sadness and wet with silent tears. "What do *you* want, Grace?"

I thought back to the brooding young man who first came into my trailer. The man before me didn't resemble him at all. Except for the dark eyes and the old soul. He wore the same dark navy suit as before with the white shirt. With my fingertips, I traced the lines of his face from his forehead to his chin. He closed his eyes, enjoying my touch.

"Just you," I replied.

"Well, I'd say you have everything you want, but I'm yours until the end of time," he said. So, mushy romantic. I wouldn't have him any other way.

"I just needed to be in the right frame of mind," I said.

"I think you need to get laid. Let go of some of the frustration. You can take it out on me." He grinned and I poked him in the ribs.

"Jenny would kill us."

"They said no kissing. Doesn't mean we can't do *anything* else," he suggested. Someone once said the devil went down to Georgia, but I was pretty sure that he was Texan.

"I want my last name to be Rearden," I said, skewing the conversation.

Levi froze in place with his mouth hanging open. "Wait, what?"

"I talked to Aydan, and his wisdom and youth made a lot of points. I won't be Grace Ann Bryant. I'll be Gloriana Rearden." The shock on his face was worth working through the grief and pain that lingered from Dylan's death.

As if it suddenly hit him, he lunged toward me, but just as his lips hit mine, my step-mother showed up.

"Stop!" Jenny screamed. "What am I going to do with both of you? Fucking fairies."

"We aren't fucking yet," Levi said, leaning back and slipping into a deep brood. So damn adorable. He shook his head at me knowing what I was thinking.

"And you aren't going to here," Jenny said.

"I wasn't going to do it here. I was going to at least take us to the trailer," Levi said.

"You had a plan," I said with a laugh.

"I've always got a plan to get you naked," he admitted.

"My hero," I teased.

"Enough. Levi, git!" Jenny exclaimed.

"Yes, ma'am." He stood up with the biggest grin on his face. Then I watched as he blinked out of sight.

"Are you finished here?" Jenny asked.

"I found what I was looking for," I replied.

"What was that?"

"Peace."

CHAPTER ELEVEN

JENNY TOOK MY HAND, JERKED ME OFF THE GROUND, AND WE BLINKED
to the trailer office. She dragged me up the front steps and in through
the door. Standing in what would be the living room, she waved her
hand and the room shifted to look just like my old trailer.

"What the hell?" I asked. "Why are we here?"

"You need a reminder of things," she said.

"What kind of spell is this?"

"Would you shut up for five minutes?"

"Excuse me," I muttered.

She inhaled deeply, then released the breath. "Grace, when you
moved to Shady Grove you had nothing. Jeremiah moved you here
after the break-up with Remy, which you now know was a much
bigger mess since his ex-wife ended up with Tennyson for a time.
Anyway. You immediately fell in love with a little baby girl and a dog.
You opened your heart up to the possibility of loving something other
than yourself."

"Wow! You make me sound like a great person."

"You weren't. You were a perfect fairy, but something happened
here in Shady Grove. Your eyes were opened before you even realized

how much you had overlooked in the days leading up to the moment you took the title of Queen of the Exiles."

"How did I miss all of it? I look back and think of how stupid I was not to notice."

"You didn't want to see past your own problems other than with Winnie, of course."

"And thanks to Dylan and his persistence, I opened my eyes to see what was there."

"We wouldn't be having a wedding today without him. I know this isn't the way you saw everything happening, but you are damn blessed. Levi Rearden will love you no matter how much you torture him until the day both of you cease living on this earth."

"He's a love talker," I said.

"And? So is Tennyson. I know what he went through for us to finally be together. He had other women and I had other men, but I can tell you that no one fulfills me like that man. Could you imagine your life going forward without him?"

"No, of course not, but this isn't how I saw it happening. I want Levi. I just don't want this hullabaloo." I raised my hands and stomped my foot for emphasis. Her glamour on the room faded.

"Is he not worth it?" she asked. "And you look ridiculous stomping your foot like a child. Very queenlike."

"When did you decide that you would take over this motherly role in my life?" I exclaimed.

"You've never had a mother," she said.

"And, I don't need one!"

"Apparently, you do, acting this way. Grace, it's time you put on your big girl panties and be the queen we all know you are inside. No more of this headstrong nonsense," she scolded.

"Headstrong is what has kept me alive despite losing Cohen, losing Dylan, and having all of this hidden from me for my entire life. How dare you!"

"I just don't want to see you making the same mistakes that I did!"

She had been a queen, and she did manage to muck that up. I saw what she was doing. She saw herself in me. I didn't have a lover to take me from my king, but I did have a family and a town that meant everything to me. Enough to ignore my duty. I crossed the living area of the trailer and walked into my office. A simple desk with pictures of my children on it. A picture of Dylan and Troy. I leaned on the desk and faced her.

"Jenny, I'm not you or Tennyson. My father chose me because I wasn't like all of you. Are you telling me that the headstrong, stubborn grindylow that I know blames herself for the fall of Camelot?"

"We had it all and gave it up."

"For?"

"Love."

I paced toward her and asked, "Love was your downfall?"

"Yes, you need to pay attention to your duty for the sake of everyone," she said.

"Do you think that I can't do both?"

"I think you will fail like we did."

"You failed because you turned your back on love. The connection that you had with father and Tennyson was unique and special, and instead of holding onto love, you split up. Father lost sight of it because of duty. You and Tennyson turned your backs on it out of guilt. I will hold on to love until the day I die, because it is what makes me who *I* am. My children, Levi, and this town are my reason for living and breathing."

She took my hand and we appeared inside my home which was eerily quiet. I turned to look at Jenny and she wore a green silk dress which matched her eyes. Her shoes were to die for. Tall heels with glittering emeralds covering the entire surface.

"Wow!" I exclaimed. "What are you, my fairy godmother?"

"As a matter of fact, for today, I am," she said, twirling her finger in the air.

Glittering dust swirled up around me as I felt powerful magic rise from the earth and from the air. I cocked my head sideways looking at Jenny who had never showed so much as an inkling of ability past her tentacles. Spinning around me, I felt dizzy as the cloud enveloped me. Slowly the cloud of glitter settled to the floor revealing the missing wedding dress already on my body, with a few enhancements. When I moved, sparkling snowflakes shimmered on the dress. The blue sequins were replaced with thousands of tiny sapphires and topaz. My shoes looked much like hers but were covered in opals.

"What was all of that back in the trailer?" I asked.

"No, Grace, the proper response is, 'Why, thank you, Jenny for making this beautiful dress for my wedding."

"Since when have I ever been proper?" I countered.

"Never." She smiled despite our heated conversation.

"Thank you. This is gorgeous," I said, swaying in the dress.

"I hid the dress so I could make some improvements."

"And that discussion we just had." I hated to prompt her again, but I needed to know what that was all about.

"We are standing in as Levi's parents. I had to know you were worthy of our son," she said.

"Really? You know I love Levi," I said.

"You were right, Grace. I *do* blame myself for not standing with your father and Lance together. What we had was special. Camelot was special. But so is Shady Grove. No matter what goes on in the Otherworld, this place deserves a Queen and King like you and Levi. Do not let anything tear you away from your love," she said with a slight touch to my cheek. "Arthur would be so proud of you today."

I didn't know what to say. Her test of loyalty seemed strange after all that we'd been through together. It also didn't seem like something Tennyson would do, but Jenny had always been a much more emotional person than he. She wasn't just testing me for Levi's sake. She tested me for the sake of all the Exiles and fairies who were supposed to be under my control. Despite the sadness of remembering what could have been with Dylan, I hadn't once thought of running. No runaway brides here. If anything, I wanted to run down that aisle and finish this.

The dress swayed beneath me as if it had a mind of its own. I brushed it down with my hands nervously. The enormity of what I was about to do settled on my shoulders.

"Thank you for everything, Jenny. I can't imagine my mother could or would have done better, wherever she is," I said, thinking about the recent revelations about my mother.

"For that matter, I'm proud of you too," she said. "Ready to get married?"

"As I'll ever be," I replied.

She offered her hand to me, and I took it. We blinked into the forest near the stone circle.

CHAPTER TWELVE

AYDAN WAITED FOR US, AND HIS EYES LIT UP IN THE DARKNESS WHEN HE saw me. He held his hand out to me, and I took it, basking in the familiar smile that matched his father's.

"Mom, you look great. Levi is going to die," he said.

"Gosh! I hope not," I said.

"My bet is on fainting," Jenny said.

"Unfortunately, I could totally see that," I said with a laugh.

"I'm going to take my place. Good luck," Jenny said with a wink and made her way to the stone circle.

"You won't believe all the people that are here," Aydan whispered. "Like the whole town."

"Well, I expected that. I suppose."

"Oh, and Grace," Jenny called back. "You supply the crown."

I sighed. I knew a crown would be a part of this. I chose the iridescent crystal one that I wore that didn't have the unicorn horn. I closed my eyes, pulling on Winter. The crown appeared on my head. Aydan looked at it in awe.

"Winnie is wearing her crown," he said.

I turned to him and ran my hand through his thick sandy hair. "You need one as well, Aydan, son of Gloriana, Queen of the Exiles."

"I don't think…" He barely got the words out of his mouth when a crown appeared on his head. Two platinum wings joined just above his brow and stretched around to each side of his head. Simple and elegant.

"Do you want to see?" I asked.

"Yes," he said, enthusiastically.

I lifted my hand, conjuring a dark plank of ice which reflected his image. He touched it lightly.

"It won't break," I said.

"Thank you, Mom," he said with glittering blue eyes.

"I know that you know I'm marrying Levi because I love him. I know that you know I am also marrying him to protect you from becoming the heir to the Winter throne. It isn't because I think you couldn't handle it, but because I want to protect you just a little while longer."

"I think I'm supposed to be upset about that, but I'm not. There are still things about this world that I don't understand," he admitted.

"You are wise beyond your years," I said as a Celtic melody began to play inside the circle. I still couldn't see inside, but we weren't too far from the edge. Winnie stood with my maid of honor waiting for us to arrive. Flowers formed a crown on Betty's white hair as she held Winnie's hand.

"I'm too old for this," she said, still protesting. When I asked her to be my maid-of-honor, she said no because she was married and old. I told her that I didn't care. She had been my first and best friend since I moved into Shady Grove. To have her by my side was an honor.

"Stop. You look beautiful," I said.

"Momma, your dress is so pretty now," Winnie exclaimed. "And Aydan has a crown!" She was so adorably excited.

"You ready, Pumpkin?" I asked.

"Yes, ma'am! I've got this flower girl thing down now. I'm an expert," she declared.

Betty nodded to me, then turned toward the circle. She carried a bouquet of white roses that contrasted with her cobalt blue gown.

When she stepped inside the circle, she disappeared. Someone had put up a ward around the circle.

Hearing a noise to my right, I turned to see a wolf's eyes glinting in the twilight. Troy had a patrol set-up to keep an eye on the perimeter. I was blessed to have so many capable hands.

"Your turn, Sis," Aydan instructed.

"I know. I know!" Winnie replied. She stepped up to the circle and walked through tossing rose petals. She too disappeared within the circle.

"Are you ready?" Aydan asked.

"I am." I smiled at him. He guided me forward, but as I suspected, this wedding would not go off without interruption. I heard a grunt behind me and turned quickly to see who it was. Aydan stepped in front of me spreading his hands out trying to block me from attack.

The smoky voice chuckled at Aydan's display. "No need to fret there, little Mr. Riggs."

"Chris Purcell, you scared us. What are you doing out here?" I asked.

The were-hog stepped out of the shadows and an orange glow illuminated his face as he puffed on a cheroot. He seemed to be dressed in wedding finery but Chris always had a swanky style about him.

"You should know that there are beings at the border to the south. I was patrolling before I came here," he said.

"What are they?" I asked.

"Wild," he replied. "They aren't moving on the barrier around the town."

"*Grace?*" Levi's concerned voice filled my head.

"*Don't worry. I'm not backing out. Chris Purcell is out here. He says there are Wild fairies patrolling the southern side of the town barrier,*" I informed him.

"*Get inside the circle, Grace. Let's do this before they attack,*" he said.

"*We should send someone,*" I replied.

"*I'll tell Troy. Let him handle it,*" he said, sounding frustrated.

"*I'm coming, Bard. Don't get your panties in a wad,*" I replied.

"*You better not be coming without me,*" he replied to lighten the tone.

"Levi is telling Troy so we can scout it out," I told Chris. "Thank you for the information."

"You're welcome, Miss Grace. Now go in there and get yourself hitched," Chris replied. "I'll finish my smoke before I join the ceremony."

Aydan brushed off his fear, but it had been real there, for a moment. His instinct was to protect me, but it scared the shit out of him.

"*Starting tomorrow, you need to train my son to fight,*" I said.

"*Don't make me come out of this circle to get you,*" he teased.

"Shake it off, Aydan."

"I'm good." He still seemed a little off, but we moved toward the tall stones anyway.

CHAPTER THIRTEEN

As I stepped inside the circle, the stones reacted to my presence. They began to glow with bright blue runes that illuminated the crowd who had turned toward us. A trio of instrumentalists played a Celtic tune off to one side. My eyes locked on Levi who swallowed hard, then mouthed, "Wow."

A wide grin spread across my face to see his appreciation. Aydan began to escort me past the entire town including some people that I knew lived here, but rarely saw. As we passed each row, the men knelt, and the women curtseyed low.

I passed the smiling faces of the people who had become family to me. But my focus stayed on Levi who stood in awe. Next to him, Dominick wore a navy-blue suit and tie. Callum also stood up with them dressed the same way. Betty and Winnie waited on my side of the officiant. Only then did I realize who Jenny had gotten to marry us.

Seamus Daragh stood in the center with a devilish grin. Levi and he stood on a wooden platform that sat in front of the center triquetra stone. When we reached the platform, Aydan paused. Nestor stood up from the front row and stepped up beside him. Tennyson stood up and stood on my opposite side.

The music stopped and the crowd was seated.

"Why is the vampirate marrying us?" I asked.

"He's a captain and this platform is made from planks of his ship," Levi replied.

"Well, I'll be damned." Jenny's creativity astounded me.

"Welcome friends and family for this momentous occasion. Now the circle will be consecrated," Seamus said in a business-like tone.

Wendy walked forward carrying a single, white pillar candle. She moved from the center to the outer edges of the circle, chanting as she made her way around the circumference. When she completed the circle, she bowed to us, then returned to her seat next to Fordele.

"Levi Rearden, Royal Bard of Winter, King of the Exiles, who presents you to this woman?"

Tennyson spoke, "I, Lancelot, Knight of the Round Table, and my beloved, Guinevere, present our god-son, Levi Rearden to be married." He patted Levi on the shoulder then returned to Jenny's side.

"Gloriana, Queen of the Exiles, Heir to the Throne of Winter, Daughter of Oberon, who presents you to this man?" Seamus asked.

"I, Nestor Gwinn, her grandfather, along with her children, Aydan, Callum, and Wynonna, present this woman to be married," Nestor said. He leaned across Aydan and kissed me on the cheek. Aydan squeezed my hand, then offered it to Levi. Levi stepped forward with his eyes on me and took my hand. Aydan didn't let go.

"Final warning, Bard," Aydan said.

"I gotcha, Bird," Levi responded with a smile. Aydan squeezed my hand again, then finally let go. With Levi's help, I stepped up on the platform next to him.

"I have never seen anything more beautiful in my entire life. You are more than beautiful. I just don't have a word for it right now," Levi said.

I blushed at his words. It wasn't just the sweetness of them, but the tone in which he spoke them in my head. It was an encompassing description of not only how I looked, but how I looked presenting myself to him to be married. The beauty wasn't just the dress, but the situation in which we stood.

Less than two years ago, Levi walked into my life. Actually, it was more begrudgingly dragged, but I tried to make him feel at home from the beginning. I saw the goodness in him. No matter what happened to him in the Otherworld, his heart still overflowed with that goodness. It may have matured him into the man standing beside me, but the pureness of his spirit remained. That pureness I could feel in the tingle of his touch. I'd said from the first touch that his was different. We knew now that the piece of me inside of him might have made the difference, but I chose to believe it was his indomitable nobility and character.

I tried reasoning with myself after the meeting with the girls about deserving his love. His devotion. I couldn't reconcile myself with it, however, I decided to accept the fact that he deserved whatever he wanted. God bless him. It was me.

"Gloriana, pledge yourself to Levi," Seamus instructed. "Unless you've changed your mind about me." The devil whispered the last part which made Levi and I laugh.

I shook my head at him, then took a deep breath.

"Levi, you have stood beside me from the moment we met. You've challenged me. You've been the voice of reason, but more than anything you have loved every part of me. The foul-mouthed part." He flashed me a devious grin as I spoke, and I almost lost my nerve. "The stubborn part. Even the darkness. I'm sorry that I didn't see you as my equal when you came here. You stuck through all of it. So, I promise to love every part of you. The kind heart. The fierce loyalty. The broods and the smiles. I promise to love you forever." The grin faded and his eyes glossed over. Something about forever stuck with him. I meant every word of it. From this day forward, it was us.

"Levi, pledge yourself to Gloriana," Seamus prompted.

Levi cleared his throat and took a deep breath. "Forever." He paused and swallowed again. "Forever is a long damn time. I gave you my forever the moment I saw the *real you* filled with power and love. I told myself it was a passing infatuation. I told myself that I wasn't man enough. But my heart told me to keep going through it all. My heart was right when my brain cast doubts. And the crazy thing is, I learned to listen to my heart by watching you. The stubbornness. The darkness. I wasn't your equal when I came here, but my heart was. The rest of me had to catch up to it. Forever is the perfect word. I promise to love you forever."

A tear rolled down my cheek. Levi reached up and brushed it away with his thumb, then pressed his thumb to his lips. Foolish, romantic man. No wonder I couldn't help myself when it came to loving him. How could I not?

Seamus allowed our words to sink into the crowd. I heard more than one sniffle, but I didn't dare to look to see who it was. The vampirate held out his hand to Callum who laid two rings in his palm.

"These look like handcuffs to me, which would be fun," Seamus said, and the crowd laughed, but Jenny cleared her throat. "Um, right. Rings symbolize undying love. Levi, take the band and place it on her finger."

Levi took the band from Seamus. We hadn't chosen bands like most couples do, so I was interested in what they looked like. As Levi slid it on my finger, I could see the triquetra pattern repeated over and over around the band. Levi twisted it once it met the engagement ring. The pattern lit up in a brilliant blue and I could feel his power running through the ring, like music for my soul. I looked up at him with wonder. His denim blue eyes flashed with the same musical power.

"This ring represents my love for you. Forever," Levi said.

Seamus offered the other ring to me. I took it and placed it on Levi's finger. I turned it in the same fashion he had. It pulsed with the same blue power, but I saw him shiver.

"This ring represents my love for you, Forever," I repeated to him.

"These two having pledged their love to each other and exchanging rings as an example now will spread the light of their love to all of you."

Winnie walked forward carrying two white candles. She closed her eyes tightly and with the cutest grunt, the flames erupted on the candles. She handed one to Levi, then the other to me.

"Great job, Wildfire," I said. She smiled with pride.

Levi and I walked hand in hand to Tennyson and Jenny who held candles of their own. We lit theirs, then moved to Nestor and Aydan. Once our family's candles flickered, they spread the fire to everyone around them until the whole circle was filled with the light which had started with us.

"You are all witnesses of this promise of love and devotions. I challenge you to support them as they go forward with the tasks ahead. Do not waver, because I know that their love won't," Seamus said.

Levi and I stepped back up on the wooden platform, then Seamus moved to the side. Levi stepped up on the center stone which came to life with his touch. He helped me stand on the stone with him. The power of the Otherworld sank into our bodies as I faced him. He wrapped his arms around me and said, "I've waited for this moment all my life."

"I've been waiting longer," I said.

"You win," he replied.

"By the power given to me as the captain of this ship," Seamus said with a stomp on the wood. "And the wonderfulness of the internet, I pronounce you husband and wife. Levi, you better kiss her good. I like to live vicariously."

Levi and I didn't pay him any attention. I was lost in the enormous power welling up around us from the Otherworld. A statement that we were coming to take back what belonged not only to me, but to him too.

"Damn. What are you waiting on? Kiss her!" Dominick teased.

Levi's forehead met mine and his fingers wrapped around my neck. I held my breath anticipating the kiss. My lips craved his touch, and I felt myself tremble in his arms. He smirked slightly then pressed his lips to mine. I opened my mouth welcoming him into it. His fingers dug into my neck as I drank him in. Lost in his kiss, I didn't notice that the power of the stone had lifted us off the ground. His tattoo erupted in the song he played only for me. Snow swirled around in the blue mist swirling around us. He released my lips and sighed.

"Do we have to go to the reception?" he asked.

I tilted my head back and laughed as our feet touched back down on the stone.

"Ladies, Gentlemen, Fairies, Shifters, and everyone else, may I present King Levi and Queen Gloriana Rearden," Seamus announced.

The crowd erupted in cheers and applause. Winnie ran up to us and hopped on the stone. Levi picked her up.

"You were floating like when Belle kisses the beast," Winnie said.

"Your mother is the beast," Levi quipped.

If he hadn't been holding my child, I would have knocked him off the stone. He knew it, too. Levi and I stepped off the stone and Callum embraced me first.

"I'm so happy for you, Mom," he said. I kissed his cheek. Then Aydan hugged me without saying a word.

Suddenly, we were surrounded by our family and friends with smiles and congratulations.

CHAPTER FOURTEEN

ASTOR, TENNYSON, AND LEVI OPENED PORTALS FOR EVERYONE TO PASS through from the circle to the reception just outside our house. We held it in the same way we had for Ella and Astor's wedding. Only instead of blending into the background, Levi and I were center stage. He and I were the last to step through our portal. When we did, the crowd cheered again. Jenny waved us to the center of the gathering where a large dance floor waited for us. When we reached the center, I looked around at the wonderful people of the town who had showed up to celebrate our day including Cletus and Tater. Flashes of their lap dances scarred my mind.

Astor stood up before the group. "Thank you all for coming to this momentous occasion. The day Grace Ann Bryant decided to give it to just one man." The crowd laughed, and my jaw dropped. Evil knight! "Now that she wants to kill me, I'd like to present a gift to her from her knights." I hadn't noticed that a white sheet covered something hanging on the wall of the reception tent behind him. He pulled a cord and the covering fell to the floor, revealing a coat of arms.

The center shield was flanked by a stag on one side and a unicorn on the other. Two snowflakes and a crown were at the top of the shield. The center of the emblem was my triquetra with a slight change. Instead of the knot forming a circle around the tri-pointed knot, a heart joined with the symbol which shimmered like a blue-green opal. In a banner across the bottom it read, "Croí Roinnte," which meant "Shared Heart" in Irish.

"That's amazing," Levi said, reaching for Astor's hand. The knight took his hand, and they patted each other on the shoulder. Then, Astor knelt before him. One by one, each of my knights knelt before Levi. Tennyson, Dominick, Troy, Astor, Finley, and Luther bowed their heads to the legitimate king. Levi pulled a small dagger out of his suit. Each man cut their hand with the dagger swearing the blood oath to him as they had to me. I walked to each one pulling power from the world around me and healing their hands finishing with Levi. He clasped my hand in his as I healed it. Then, he lifted it to his lips with a smile.

"I guess I have to keep you now," I said.

"You are stuck with me," he replied.

"I'll manage somehow."

The knights moved back into the crowd, and the next person to appear by our side was Seamus. "I think we should start this party off with a dance by the King and Queen."

The crowd cheered, the lights dimmed, and Levi escorted me back to the center of the space. I saw no musicians and knew he'd be playing the song. I looked around at the people watching us and became nervous with all the eyes on me. He placed his finger on my chin, lightly turning my head back to him.

"This is just you and me," he said.

"Right," I agreed.

Wrapping his arm around my waist, he pulled me to his body. Suddenly, I felt his magic move with no song. A calming spell during which I shook my head at him. He captured my free hand with his and brought it to his chest near his heart. The guitar came to life playing a sweet, slow melody that seemed familiar. A song that I'd heard on the radio. The only lyrics I remembered was something about loving someone for a thousand years. I knew I'd love Levi for many more than that. Even if my death came, I'd take the piece of his heart he'd given me with me. He already had mine. All of it.

We swayed slowly to the music, and I stared into his eyes. Strong and confident, they reflected back to me about the man he'd become. The man that had waited patiently for my love to catch up with his. We didn't speak at all during the dance. Levi believed in me, and more importantly, he believed in us. I'm not sure I ever would have if he hadn't fought for it. The love talker in him had many skills, but Levi had always been a kind soul. You could see it in those deep blue eyes. That kindness spoke to me.

Moving closer to him, I laid my head on his chest, and he sighed. The tingle between us had not quit from the moment we first touched. It had strengthened over time, but we were both used to it now. However, changing with the intensity of our relationship, the tingle had become more of a hum. Levi called it our symphony. I teased him saying it was made of kazoos, but he shrugged it off. I was sure that he heard horns, strings, and drums.

When the dance ended, he held me tightly.

"I love you, Grace."

"I love you too, Dublin."

Pulling away from him was the signal to our guests that they could besiege us with congratulations and best wishes. We spoke to everyone that came to wish us well. Tater and Cletus hugged me with enthusiasm.

"Miss Grace, you are looking finer than a frog's hair split three ways," Cletus said.

"Cletus, she looks better than a frog!" Tater protested.

"I said frog's hair!" Cletus countered.

"She looks better than frog's hair!" Tater came back. "Did you see what we made for ya?"

"No, I didn't," I replied. Honestly, I was a little afraid to ask what it was. Tater grabbed my hand and towed me across the dance floor, through a bunch of tables to the buffet. At the end of the table, a large blue plastic swimming pool rested. A second tier was added with a smaller version of the bottom pool. The center tower was made of aluminum cans. The whole contraption was pumping out an orangey liquid.

"Ain't it great?!" Cletus said.

Levi stood behind me snickering.

"It's a fountain," I muttered not knowing what else to call it.

"It's a Trailermosa Fountain," Tater countered.

"What is Trailermosa?" I asked.

"Why it's the grandest drink in the whole trailer park. We thought you'd love it because it's made with orange soda," Cletus said, sounding a little disappointed in my level of enthusiasm.

"Oh, well, I do love orange soda. What's it mixed with? Vodka? Champagne?" I asked.

"Hell, no. In the trailer park, we use beer!" Tater proudly proclaimed. "We don't need none of that fancy shit."

"Wanna try some?" Cletus asked, picking up a cup and placing it under one of the drilled holes in the side of the swimming pool.

"I do!" Levi said behind me. "Come on, Grace! Try some."

"I'm gonna knock you into next week," I grumbled under my breath.

"I'd rather you fuck me into next week," he grumbled back taking the cup from Cletus. He took a sip and shrugged. "Tastes great to me. Here, have a sip."

I took a deep breath and took a sip of the concoction from Levi's cup. All I tasted was beer. I hated beer. It took everything I had not to spit it out. Levi laughed at the scowl on my face, and I stuck my tongue out at him.

"I'll let you use that later," he said. Cletus and Tater heard him say it, and they whooped and laughed. I just shook my head and looked for something to cleanse my palate. Thankfully, Betty saved me.

"Here, this is more your speed," she said, handing me a glass of honey brown liquid. I took a sip of the whiskey, and suddenly I felt much better. "Just look at that monstrosity." We stared at the Trailermosa fountain while Cletus and Tater handed out cups of the drink to everyone. Tennyson walked up to Levi, drawing his attention away from me.

"It's perfect," I said with a smile. "A little piece of the trailer park here at our reception."

"There was no talking them out of it. Luther had to go fetch another table just for it," Betty said, taking a sip of her own honey brown liquid. "Come look at the rest of the spread."

In the center of the table a four-tier cake rose up above all the other food. It looked like a work of art. Luther knew I loved wedding cake. Plain white cake and white icing, which this was, but the white icing was covered in sparkling snowflakes and some sort of white cotton candy- looking stuff swirling around it. On top of the cake, a replica of the coat of arms sat in a simplified form. Just the stag and unicorn on each side of the shield with the heart triquetra.

"The cake is amazing!" I gushed.

"Why, thank ya, Grace," Luther said behind me. I turned, giving him a huge hug.

"I'll tolerate you hugging my man, just this once," Betty quipped.

"Just this once, I thank ya," I replied

One end of the table was filled with savory treats including mini biscuits with gravy dipping sauce. There were other treats like bowls of nuts from the Hot Tin Roof, cheeseburger sliders, mini-BBQ sandwiches from Brad's place, and some other fried balls.

"What are those?" I asked.

"Well, that's something I concocted," Luther confessed.

"Hope it isn't like a Trailermosa," I said.

He laughed. "No, nothing that grand. It's little deep-fried balls of spaghetti, since it is your family's favorite meal."

"Well, we do deep-fry everything in the south," I said. "Some of them look different."

"Some of them are mac and cheese for Winnie," Luther replied.

"I helped with those," Aydan said behind me.

"Well, you can start doing the cookin' around the house," I said, giving him a hug, too.

"Luther is teaching me. It's fun," he replied.

I suppose if Aydan wanted to be a cook or a chef, I would be just fine with that.

On the sweet end of the table, I spied Mrs. Frist's famous fudge and some pink cookies.

"What kind of cookies are those?" I asked.

"They are strawberry milkshake cookies," Betty said. "You probably drank your weight in them when you were pregnant."

"I wasn't eating anything else, but I could definitely drink those," I said, taking a bite of one of the cookies. It was like it transformed in my mouth from a cookie into a cool blast of strawberry ice cream. "Oh, wow!"

"Mike gave me a liquid that allows them to transform once you eat them," Luther said proudly.

"That's fuckin' amazing!" I said, grabbing another. "Winnie, come try these cookies."

Winnie ran up with Mark in her shadow. I handed one to each of them. As they took their bites, I watched their eyes light up.

"Oh, my goodness, that's awesome," Winnie exclaimed.

Mark looked confused. "What kind of cookies are these?"

"Strawberry milkshake," I replied.

He took another bite, then nodded his head as if he liked them, but I wasn't sure. He looked up to me with questioning eyes.

"What is it?" I asked.

"May I dance with Winnie?" he asked.

"Mark, if you want to dance with Winnie, then you should ask Winnie," I said.

"I just wanted to make sure it was okay with you," he replied.

"Whatever she wants," I answered.

"Thank you, ma'am. Miss Wynonna Riggs, will you please dance with me?" he asked boldly.

Winnie stopped chewing her cookie and looked at me, then back at him. I nodded to her hoping she wouldn't leave him hanging. She wiped her hands on her dress, and I bit my lip. "Why, yes, Mark Maynard, I will dance with you," she responded.

Mark released a sigh. I supposed it was a relief that she didn't blast him for asking. She was more my child every day. Levi walked up to me, as we watched the two kids walk to the dance floor like a couple of adults.

"He's a good kid," Levi said.

"Yeah, but she's a wildfire," I replied.

"If he loves her, he will stick through it," Levi said.

"Is that supposed to mean something?" I asked him with a tease.

"Just means the best things come to those who wait," he replied.

The gypsy band began to play and many of our friends danced with our children.

"What's wrong?" I asked Levi who seemed more tense after his talk with Tennyson.

"We have trouble," he replied.

"Don't we always?"

"Yes, but we are going to deal with it after the party."

"Does it need to be handled now?"

He looked at me with tense eyes. The news he had gotten was serious. "We will celebrate our marriage, then we will deal with it."

I nodded, but it had my senses buzzing. If it were immediate trouble, we would deal with it now, but apparently, we had time to finish this out.

"Let's cut the cake!" Betty exclaimed.

Levi and I went through the ritual of cutting the cake and taking a thousand pictures. We managed to feed each other cake without any of the rude smashing, no matter how much I really wanted to rub icing on his nose.

"Speech! Speech!" someone in the crowd called out. Others echoed the call.

"You are the bard. Go ahead," I said.

Levi grabbed a nearby chair and stood on it. The crowd clapped, but he motioned for them to get quiet.

"Thanks for being here to celebrate this occasion. It means everything to Grace and me to have our exile family here with us. I know there are dark days ahead, but I assure you that we will fight as we have never fought. We will become the dark, cunning fairies they expect us to be. If we are a bunch of misfits, then so-fucking-be-it!" The crowd cheered. "Somebody give me a trailermosa!" Cletus obliged him. He raised the glass high. "Here's to being the best badasses this side of the Otherworld!"

Cheers and enthusiastic agreement erupted across the guests. They lifted their glasses and drank down the horrid concoction with spirit. I took a gulp of my whiskey. Levi had roused the crowd with such a simple speech. His power for words exceeded my expectations of what a bard could do. He once wondered if he could control a crowd. I had no doubts now. More importantly, neither did he.

He climbed down from the chair, then scooped me up for a passionate kiss which pleased the already rowdy crowd.

"Good job," I said, grinning at him.

"It was alright." He knew it was good. So humble.

The musicians began to play again, and everyone mingled in a jolly mood.

We were talking to Eugene and Chaz when Dominick walked up.

"Congratulations," he said.

"Thank you," I replied.

"So, how about I get that dance now?" he asked. "I asked Levi first." "And?"

"I said he could ask," Levi replied.

"You don't have to, Grace. Just bringing up silly memories," Nick said.

"I'd be honored," I replied.

Chaz choked on his cake, and Gene patted him on the back. I rolled my eyes at him, and looked at Levi before I took Nick's arm. He nodded.

"*I'm pretty sure you owe him a dance anyway,*" he said.

"*I probably do,*" I replied. "*Because he saved your ass in Summer.*"

"*That's not what I meant!*" Levi protested.

I took Nick's arm with a smile, and he took me to the dance floor. He made very sure he didn't hold me too tightly as we danced to the gypsy band's slow ballad. Holding his hand, I couldn't even tell it was a glamour. Nick's fairy power tingled only slightly as I touched him.

He'd barely touched his potential, but he seemed content with what he had. There was no need to push it.

"Thank you for taking care of him in Summer," I said.

"Oh, so that is why you said yes."

"No, I said yes because I wanted to."

"Well, hot damn. You are welcome. Levi is like the brother I never had. I know that I love him like that. We've had our differences, but I think we both realized that it was your fault," Nick teased.

"Well, bless your hearts," I smirked.

He tilted his head back and laughed. "I love ya both like family," he said seriously.

"You know you are always welcome in our home," I replied.

"When I left my father's house, I was resigned to be a loner for the rest of my life. I knew that I had very little chance of finding happiness, but being here and being a part of Shady Grove has surpassed anything I ever dreamt of. Thank you for sticking with me when it got rough."

"That's what we do. We haven't seen the worst of it though," I said.

"No, we haven't, but it's better to face it together, than alone."

"So much better," I replied as the music stopped. He leaned in and kissed my cheek.

"Thank you for the dance," he said with a handsome smile. He ran his hand through his disheveled hair, then backed away into the crowd of people.

CHAPTER FIFTEEN

My dance with Dominick marked the end to the normal wedding. Before I could exit the dance floor, I heard frantic barking from the other side of the gathering. I knew it had to be Rufus. I rushed over to where he was with Levi joining me once we got there. The little dog would not give up no matter how much I coaxed him. He enthusiastically barked at a bush.

"Oh no!" a shrill voice behind me exclaimed.

Bramble fluttered by me like a dart followed by Briar. They slammed into the bush just outside the back porch of my house. Rufus continued to bark.

"Rufus, hush!" I scolded him. He whimpered, but ceased his alert.

Levi stepped up to the bush, pushing it apart. "Shit," he muttered. "Tennyson!"

The knight pushed his way through the crowd to our side.

"What is it, Levi?" he asked.

"Thistle," Levi said, slowly pulling his hands from out of the limbs of the bush. Her normally purple hair was black, and her body laid limply in Levi's hand. Bramble cried profusely, and Briar patted his head as tears rolled down her cheeks.

"Is she dead?" I asked.

"Yes, my sweet little love muffin has passed from this cruel world," Bramble lamented.

Winnie and Mark started to approach. "Mark, you and Winnie stay over there," I instructed. I didn't want Winnie to see the poor little thing. "Was she out working for you?" I asked Tennyson.

"She was," he grumbled.

"Where?" I asked.

"In Winter," he replied. "I should have pulled her out, but she insisted. She was bringing back important information."

Wendy joined us with Artemis. Remington Blake was close on her heels. I guessed he'd found someone to mend his wounds.

"May I?" Artemis asked, holding up her hands.

Levi carefully handed Thistle's body over to Artemis.

"Let's take her inside where there is more light and away from the party," I said, as Jenny walked up. "Could you stay out here with the guests?"

"Sure, Grace. Just keep me informed," Jenny replied.

We hustled into the house, and I grabbed a dish towel from the sink. I folded it several times creating a soft spot for the little brownie's body. Artemis felt Thistle's arms and chest using just the tips of her fingers.

"I don't think there is anything I can do. She's gone," Artemis said, backing away from the makeshift bed.

Tennyson groaned. "I shouldn't have sent her back."

"She wanted to go back," Levi said.

"How do you know that?" I asked.

"She came in last night to Tennyson's cabin with information about a leader in Winter with a legitimate claim to the throne. Someone that could challenge you," Levi explained.

"I sent her back to find out exactly who it is," Tennyson said.

"Did you compel her or force her to do it?" I asked.

"No. She always loved being my little spy. Going back was her idea," he said. "She only came out to give me the info."

"And this is what we needed to talk about later?" I asked.

"Yes, and other things," Levi said.

"Now is the time," I said.

Levi grimaced, realizing that our celebration had reached its end. We had made a good go of it, but there were more important things going on.

"We knew that Brockton had married someone in Winter. We just assumed it was Robin or one of Rhiannon's other daughters. He married whomever this person is, that is claiming rights to your father's throne," Tennyson explained. His face looked worn and tired. The brownie's death weighed heavily on his heart.

"Who is it? A woman? A man?" I asked.

"We aren't sure. I'll send in other spies," Tennyson said.

"Finley offered to go," I said.

"We should get the knights in here," Tennyson suggested.

"I'll gather everyone," Levi said.

"Don't stop the party, Levi. The town needs it," I said.

He nodded, then slipped out the back door. I took out a plastic container from the cabinet and placed the dish towel and tiny body inside. I didn't put a lid on it but placed another towel over the top of it. The last thing I wanted was for Winnie to come in and find the dead body. Granted Winnie was more attached to Bramble and Briar, but this would hurt her little heart. Aydan and Callum came in the backdoor.

"What's going on?" Aydan asked.

"Thistle is dead," I said. "Please keep an eye on your sister. Don't let her out of your sight. Keep her out of here for now. And if you see Bramble and Briar, send them upstairs so they don't frighten Winnie."

"How terrible," Callum said. "Come on, Aydan." The boys went back out in search of their sister. I watched through the window as my knights quietly slipped away from the party and into the house.

I realized that Artemis and Remy still stood in the kitchen. "Will you do me a favor, too?"

"Of course, Grace," Remy replied.

"Go out there and spread the rumor that Levi and I decided to start the honeymoon early or something. Keep the party going."

"We can do that," Artemis said, moving to the back door.

"You looked beautiful today, Gracie. I wish you all the best," Remy said.

I walked up and kissed him on the cheek. "Thank you, Remington Blake."

He blushed, then followed Artemis out the door.

* * *

THE KNIGHTS WERE GATHERED around my living room while the town partied outside. I sat with Levi in the recliner while Tennyson, Jenny, and Troy sat on the couch. Dominick and Luther sat in chairs from the dining room. Astor sat in the other living room chair. Nestor stood in the darkness of the kitchen, silently observing. Finley sat on the floor near the front door.

"Is there any other information about this mysterious heir?" I asked.

"We have plenty of brothers," Finley said.

"Brockton is fairy. He very well could have a male lover or husband," I said.

"No, he would want someone he could control," Tennyson said.

"Males can be dominated as much as females," I smirked.

"True dat," Jenny added.

"Okay. Let's think about this. Brockton took the Otherworld using Stephanie as a pawn. The witches who are the former Queens seem to be on either side to destabilize whatever they can. Stephanie and Tabitha are now living here as reincarnated exiles with wiped memories. Is Titania out there somewhere? They tried taking me out more than once. They tried destroying me by taking Dylan, by taking Levi, and by triggering the events that led to Dylan's death. They have untold amounts of Wild Fairies fighting for them. Am I missing anything?"

"Demetris Lysander tried to take you out," Nestor said from the kitchen.

"That's when all of this shit started," I thought out loud.

"Why did Demetris turn on your father? For many years, I thought he was a loyal servant," Tennyson said.

"Oh, my goddess," I said. I stood up and paced the room.

"Grace, what is it?" Levi urged.

"You were there in the stone circle when Jeremiah told us why Lysander hated me," I said to him.

"Oh, shit," he muttered.

"Oh, shit, what?" Tennyson growled.

"Lysander's daughter was one of my father's concubines. She had a daughter by my father who he did not accept as an heir," I said.

"No, you were the only daughter," Finley said.

"That's not what Jeremiah told us," I said.

"She's right. I remember it now. He was trying to get Grace to take on her role as Queen of the Exiles. Grace thought it was just because she'd turned Lysander down so many times," Levi said.

"I'm telling you. There were no other daughters," Finley repeated.

"Was it possible that because he didn't claim her that she would be exiled like me? Or her mother perhaps? She might be living in this town or had at one point." My thoughts poured out of my mouth, but Levi's came to me in my head.

"It's Lisette," he said.

"No."

"Yeah. Lysander was an Aswang. He was Wild, not Unseelie. Your father had a daughter with a Wild fairy. And I slept with her," he groaned.

"Oh please. I've got a whole line of people I shouldn't have slept with. You are right. It's Lisette. It's why she is so powerful. She's part Wild, and part royal Unseelie."

"Y'all can clue us into this conversation whenever you are ready," Nick smirked.

"It's Lisette," Levi said for everyone to hear this time. "It has to be."

"She's a descendant of the Wild King. The Erlking. Not the Winter King," Tennyson said.

"Lysander was Aswang. His daughter had a daughter with my father, according to Jeremiah. Someone get Caiaphas here. He will tell us what he knows." Luther walked to the front door, and I heard his wings ignite as he stepped off the porch. "That would make Lysander part of the Wild Royalty. It would make him what, the Erlking or the Erlking's son?"

Tennyson still shook his head. "There is no way I missed something this big." Jenny gently rubbed his shoulders.

"So, what if she is your Father's daughter? Her claim cannot be as strong as yours," Troy said.

"Actually, she is the heir to the Wild throne. The Wild served Oberon," Astor said.

"And they serve her now. If she is married to Brockton, then one would think that he could control them," I added. "It's why there are so many there. It makes sense."

Luther came back in the door and sat back down in his seat. I had no idea that the Ifrit could fly so fast.

"Luther?" Levi asked.

"Caiaphas is dead," he said.

"Son of a bitch!" I screamed. "Fucking Kady."

"We don't know that's who killed him," Troy said.

"He's been dead a day or so," Luther said.

"How do you kill Merlin?" Levi asked.

"He doesn't have that power anymore," I said, sitting back down on the recliner with him. Levi placed his hand on my back, sending vibrating pulses of magic into me. I didn't know what it was, but I trusted that he would do whatever he could to help me.

"How do we find out for sure?" Levi asked.

"Someone has to go, and I'll do it," Tennyson said.

"No, I've already told you I was going," Finley said. "I can get in and out. Is that all we need? Verify that Lisette is married to Brockton?"

"Yes. That is the most important thing," Tennyson said.

"We need to have a good estimate on how many Wild troops they have," Astor suggested.

"Lisette was from Louisiana, right?" Nick asked.

"Yes," Levi answered.

The wheels in Nick's head turned, and I could have sworn I saw steam coming out of his ears. "I know a lot of that area. Even the swamps. There is a pack down there. We might reach out to them and see if we can get any information about her from when she was there. Where about in Louisiana?"

"She lived in a little town called Golden Meadow," Levi said. "But she spent most of her time out in the swamps when I was there."

"That's along the LaFourche Bayou. I can go down there and see what I can find out," Nick offered.

"We need you back here quickly. I'm not going to wait any longer," I said.

"Give me 24 hours," he said.

"That's quick," Levi said.

"As the wolf runs," Nick replied. "I'll get going with Troy's permission."

"You don't need my permission," Troy said.

"Good. I'll get going. Don't run off and fight without me," he said. He stopped in front of Levi and I, giving us a slight bow, then hurried out the front door. I hated to see him go, and I felt the same sentiment coming from Levi. However, we were missing pieces of the puzzle and we needed to know what we were up against going into the Otherworld.

"Hypothetically, if Lisette is a descendant of my father and the Erlking, how strong is her claim? She's married to my father's brother, too," I said.

"I'd say it's a matter of possession, Grace," Tennyson said.

"As soon as the party is over, we need to make our final preparations to move into the Otherworld," I said. "Finley, are you ready to go?"

"I need to see Riley before I head out, but otherwise, yes," he said.

"Be safe, Fin."

"Don't you worry your pretty head, Glory. I'll be back. I've got a few hundred years left in me to pester you," he said with a grin. I stood up and hugged him. He shook hands with Levi. "You know that threat from Aydan?"

"Yeah," Levi chuckled.

"That goes for me too," Fin said.

"Oh, get out of here. Nobody is going to whoop Levi's ass but me," I said.

"Sweet!" Levi exclaimed.

A tense laugh ripped across the room. Finley nodded, then slipped out the back door.

"Now what?" I asked.

"Now you go throw a bouquet and we shut the party down," Jenny said.

I couldn't have asked for a better wedding. Even as thrown together as it was, Trailermosas and all. I was happy. Levi and I could move forward as a recognized unit.

"She needs to officially give Levi the keys to the kingdom," Tennyson said. I imagined it was his code for consummating the marriage.

"I'm gonna give him a lot more than that if you people will get out of my house," I teased. It was half-hearted, but I was trying to keep their spirits up.

"The kids are going with us," Troy said.

"You don't have to do that," I said.

Troy laughed. "Yeah, we do. No need to scar them."

"Get outta here," I exclaimed.

"What about Thistle?" Astor asked.

"I'll take her. We will have a pyre built for her," Tennyson said.

I nodded as sadness overtook the mood again. With hugs and well wishes, Levi and I rejoined the party. The others joined us except for Dominick, Finley, and Tennyson. Chaz met me with my bouquet. "Now. No aiming. You have to turn your back and throw it."

The single women in town gathered on the dance floor while Levi helped me step up into a chair. Most of my single friends had gotten married already, but there were a few people I recognized. Juanita Santiago's presence made me smile. I'd killed her abusive husband for treason. Instead of causing her grief, it gave her a relief and a new purpose in life. Artemis, the wolf doctor, was pushed onto the floor by Remington Blake who stood next to his friend Niles Babineau. Jessica, the Summer fairy who used to work at the police station, boldly stepped out in a very revealing black dress that hugged her curves. She looked fantastic, and I figured that dress was better than any bouquet she could catch. BBQ Brad stood holding hands with Tonya, his beautiful ginger waitress. They were having a discussion, then she finally joined the others in the group. Crystal Marie, the were-bobcat, stepped out on the floor, and I noticed that Kwaski, the were-possum, studied her closely. I hadn't seen her since she was in Ella's wedding.

"Where is LeAnne?" The Valkryie had a way of blending in and hiding in spots I wouldn't notice.

She stepped out of the crowd in full armor. "I'm here, my Queen."

"Are you married?" I asked.

"No, but I cannot," she replied.

"Whatever! This is Shady Grove. We break the rules here," I replied with a few nods and grins from the crowd.

"I will participate if you order it," LeAnne said stoically.

"I order it," I replied as Levi shook his head.

"Very well," she said, pushing her way to the front of the group. She held the women back determined to win the prize. Nothing like a little competition.

The group of single ladies got into the spirit of things and began to push their way to the front, vying for position.

"Alright. Here I go!" I announced, turning my back to the crowd. I tossed the bouquet high into the air. Turning quickly, I watched the women push and pull trying to get under the flying flowers. At the last moment, a hand emerged from the throng, grabbing it from in front of everyone else. There was a collective groan from the losers, and the winner shocked me.

Katherine Frist grinned widely and accepted some of the congratulations from the losers. She looked around the wedding guest and called out, "Oh, Nestor!"

"No," I muttered.

"Grace, she won it fair and square," Levi scolded.

"She can't have my grandfather," I said. "He's been through enough."

Nestor appeared at the edge of the crowd with a red face. He shook his head at her, but she sauntered up to him. "Lookie what I got?" The crowd laughed, and I felt Levi gently holding me back.

"Katherine, stop this display. Please," he said, looking around. They had the full attention of everyone there.

"I got the flowers. The rest is up to you," she said as she reached him. She ran her long fingers through his hair which he wore down for the wedding. He actually looked quite handsome in his tuxedo.

"Would you stop?" he said, fighting a grin. "The last thing I want to be is another one of your dead husbands."

"I assure you they all died happy," she said, rubbing up against him.

"I'm going to puke," I whispered.

"He seems to be enjoying it," Levi said.

"Katie, please stop," Nestor begged again.

She leaned into his ear to whisper, and I concentrated on the movement of her lips to pick up her words with magic. "I promise not to kill you. I've finally found a man my equal in bed." Yep, I was going to hurl. Nestor turned magenta and grabbed her hand. He looked at me, giving me a nod, then dragged her out of the crowd into the darkness. The guests whooped and hollered, as we watched them climb in his truck and drive away.

"I'm going to be sick," I said.

"Leave him alone. She won't kill him. She knows you'd skin her alive," Levi said.

"Oh, I will do much worse."

"Calm down, Ice Queen," Levi scolded. "By the way, do I get to remove your garter?"

"I'm not sure I have on a garter. Jenny magically dressed me," I said.

"I'm willing to find out," Levi said, lifting an eyebrow.

Jenny walked up and pointed at the chair I had stood on to throw the bouquet. "You are wearing one."

I rolled my eyes, and Levi shivered with excitement. He guided me to the chair, and I hiked up my skirt to reveal a dainty lace garter with a blue ribbon and a sapphire snowflake accent.

"Oh, something blue," I said.

"Yes, I follow traditions. Your engagement ring is old. Your dress is new. That crown is borrowed, and the garter is blue," Jenny explained.

"This crown is borrowed?" I asked.

"It belongs to the Winter realm. If there ever comes a time that you aren't its Queen, it will go to the next in line," she explained.

"I suppose that is true," I said.

"That horned thing you wear is yours, but the crystalline crown belongs to the realm," she said.

"Noted," I replied. Levi looked annoyed. He was ready to put his hands up my skirt.

Astor stepped up behind Levi with a blindfold.

"What the hell is this?" Levi asked.

"You can feel your way to that garter," Astor teased.

"Watch where you are putting your hands, Ginger Snap," Levi teased back.

"You wish," Astor shot back.

"Wait a minute! I can't use my sight?!" Levi said.

"Yep. No cheating. I know a few witches!" Astor exclaimed with glee.

"Fuck!" Levi muttered.

Jenny grabbed my arm and pulled me up out of the chair. She placed her finger over her mouth to warn me to keep quiet. Cletus took my place in the chair. His lips were painted deep red. I covered my mouth before I gasped. He lifted his overall pant leg to reveal a freshly shaved leg with a dainty white garter.

"He is going to kill us!" I mouthed to Jenny.

"Not me. You," she said with an evil grin.

Astor guided Levi to the waiting Cletus, who produced a lace fan and proceeded to fan himself and make kissy faces to the crowd. "Kneel down to your Queen, Bard."

Levi obediently knelt down, reaching forward to touch Cletus' leg. The crowd cheered him on.

"*How much can I play this up?*" Levi said in my head. At first, I thought he'd caught on to the ruse, but I decided to respond as if he hadn't just in case.

"*As much as you want. Give them something to remember,*" I suggested.

With that Levi dipped his head to Cletus' offered leg and kissed it lightly.

"*Why are you so nervous?*" he asked.

"*You know me and public displays of affection,*" I replied.

"*You feel different,*" he said.

"*Must be marriage,*" I replied.

Jenny whispered in my ear. "Has he figured it out?"

I shook my head. "No, but he knows something is off."

"The kiss was worth it."

Levi ran his hands up and down Cletus' leg and I giggled for effect. I didn't know what else to do. When his hands found the garter, he leaned over it. With his teeth, he latched on to the garter.

"Levi Rearden, I never!" I exclaimed, and Jenny began to laugh uncontrollably. Astor and Troy were holding each other up because they were laughing so hard.

"Just you wait," Levi replied while Cletus continued to fan himself.

I heard Chaz comment behind me. "I never thought I'd ever be jealous of Cletus Sawyer, but there it is."

Levi pulled the garter down the leg with his teeth, then pulled it off with his hand. He leaned over the toes of Cletus' foot.

"Levi! No!" I yelled just before he put his mouth on the toes.

Levi jerked off the blindfold, then stumbled backward. His mouth fell open, and he looked back and forth from me to Cletus who fanned and twiddled his fingers at him.

"Son of a bitch," Levi said. His face was darker than a cherry.

Jenny pointed at me. "Don't you dare! You did this!" I declared.

Levi's forehead wrinkled as Astor dragged him to his feet. Levi looked at the garter in his hand and pulled it back taut. He released it and it smacked Cletus in the face. Cletus squealed like a woman. It was hilarious!

"Divorce! I want a divorce!" Cletus exclaimed.

I shook my head at the spectacle. Levi shook off the frustration, and I approached him slowly. "I didn't know. Honest."

He started to laugh and couldn't stop. "Damn. I fell for that. I didn't feel the tingle, and it never registered."

"I need you to be able to recognize me in the dark," I said.

"I'll need to practice that," he said.

"How about now?" I offered.

"No way. I want the lights on tonight," he said.

Jenny stood next to us. "It was supposed to be Dominick, but he ran off. We had to shave Cletus' leg. Trust me, you didn't get the worst of it."

"Well, I declare," Cletus said, fanning himself.

"I'll get you later," Levi said, pointing at Cletus. "And you." He pointed at Astor whose face was as red as his hair from laughter. Ella stood next to him laughing, but then she grabbed her belly.

"Ella," I said, through the commotion. Her eyes met mine, and I saw panic.

"It's time," she said as a puddle of water formed at her feet.

"Astor!" Levi said, pointing at Ella.

"Oh! Shit!" the chaste knight cursed. "What do I do?"

"Get her inside!" I exclaimed.

He went to pick her up, and she swatted at him. "I can walk. Just help me."

Levi, Jenny, and I guided her into the spare bedroom where Callum usually slept. I gave Levi instructions to get towels and blankets from upstairs. Artemis and Wendy appeared at the door.

"Y'all ready to do this again?" I asked.

"Let's do it," Wendy replied.

We rushed around the room preparing for the birth while Astor held Ella's hands through the contractions. Wendy waited patiently at the bottom of the bed where we had positioned her with a stool to assist the birth.

"Argh!" Ella exclaimed. "Oh, sweet goddess, that fucking hurts!"

"You gotta start pushing," Wendy said. "I can already see the top of a head."

"You gotta save your strength, because we gotta do it twice," I said to Ella.

"She can do it," Astor said confidently. Levi stood at the door, waiting for additional instructions. I shot him a weak smile.

"I'm sorry," I said.

"Grace, this is Shady Grove. I didn't expect this to be an event-free wedding," he said with a genuine smile.

"I love you so much," I said.

"We will have time for you to prove it," he said, and I swore his eyes darkened with mischief. I grinned at him, because I loved it.

"Push!" Wendy yelled. I waited by her side with a fresh, soft blanket that Levi had retrieved from Astor's house. The little head appeared with flashy red hair. I grinned at the sight. Just like his daddy. The boy was coming first. Always, like men, so pushy.

With a few more pushes, the screaming ginger baby boy was handed to his adoring parents.

"My heavens. I've never seen anything more beautiful," Astor cooed.

"Little conceited considering he looks just like you," Levi teased.

"Bard, it does not matter what you say to me. Nothing will bring me down from this cloud," Astor said.

"The other one is pushing," Ella grunted.

"Then push with it!" Wendy demanded.

Astor backed away with the wiggly bundle in his arms as Wendy and I prepared to catch the second one. After a couple of pushes, we hadn't made any progress.

"Is something wrong?" Levi asked.

"No, this one is just being stubborn," Wendy said.

"Just like a woman," I blurted.

"Woman?" Astor and Ella's eyes flashed to mine.

"Oops," I muttered.

"A boy and a girl?" Astor whispered in awe.

"She wasn't supposed to tell," Levi scolded.

"Sorry." I hadn't meant to tell, but I knew they were having one of each.

"We will have to rethink the names," Astor said.

"Aaaaaaaaaargh!" Ella said, pushing again.

Artemis dabbed her forehead with a damp cloth after each push. The boy had arrived within the first fifteen minutes. It took another hour and a half before the little girl appeared, but when she did, it was silently, unlike her brother. I thought Astor was going to faint again as he held both babies.

"I'm a father," Astor said.

"You are going to be a great Dad," Levi said.

I smiled at the new parents who cuddled their precious children. Levi moved from the doorway as Chaz and Eugene joined the couple. They were enamored with their grandchildren immediately.

"They are beautiful," I said as Wendy and Artemis cleaned up.

"*Baby fever?*" Levi asked.

"*Baby making fever, actually,*" I replied.

"You guys can stay here tonight and rest," Levi offered. There went my loud honeymoon.

"Thank you, my King," Astor replied. "I need to show everyone!" He grabbed the two bundles one in each of his bulky arms and trotted to the back door. We followed him down the hallway as Ella protested.

"They will be fine," Wendy coaxed her.

Levi grabbed my hand, and we ran down the hallway and out the door. The party had died down as everyone waited on news about the birth.

"My children!" Astor exclaimed.

The crowd cheered. Some came forward to see the ginger headed babies. They were adorable.

"Well, congratulations," Jenny said, peering at the babies.

"Thank you, Gwen."

Levi hugged me to his side as we watched the proud papa show off his offspring.

CHAPTER SIXTEEN

Astor and Ella discussed names while we got them settled in Callum's bedroom.

"The party is finally breaking up," Aydan said. "I'm beat."

"Me too," Callum said.

"Winnie is asleep on the couch," Aydan said.

"Do you mind taking her upstairs? You guys can just stay here tonight," I said.

"No, we can go to Troy's," Callum said.

"It's okay. I'd rather have my family here," I replied. Levi squeezed my hand in agreement.

Aydan and Callum made their way to the living room. Aydan lifted Winnie while Callum followed them up the stairs to her room.

We said good-bye to our guests, except for Tennyson and Troy who stayed behind. Even Luther had to leave. Betty insisted he spend some time in his bottle. I wondered if there wasn't more to that bottle than they let on, but now was not the time to ask.

"The children are well?" Tennyson asked.

"They are," I replied as I collapsed on the couch. I would have already taken off the wedding dress if Levi hadn't insisted that I keep it on for now. I was thankful that Wendy took on the messier part of the birth, so I wasn't covered in birthing gore. Levi sat down next to me, and I curled myself into his side.

"We will start preparing immediately. The two of you need to have some alone time," Tennyson said.

"That's going to be hard to do with a houseful of people," I replied. "It doesn't matter. I want them all at home today."

Light gradually came through the windows as Tennyson talked over the final preparations for our assault on the Otherworld. His son had gone to check the fountain, and that was why we didn't see him at the wedding.

"My wolves are still patrolling the borders. We still have would-be intruders at the gates," Troy said.

"I want to see them," I said.

"No, Grace. You and Levi need to…"

"Yeah, yeah. I gotcha, but this needs to be handled," I said.

Levi sighed, because he knew I wasn't going to back down. That's why I married him. He knew when to keep his mouth shut.

"Where is the biggest group of them?" Levi asked.

"At the south highway," Troy said.

"Alright. Let's go," I said.

Tennyson created a portal for Levi, Troy, and me to walk through. We stepped into the early dawn in the forest just off the main south highway that led out of town. At the border, I saw about 30 wild fairies gathered. A couple of trolls, bogans, red caps, and one big guy that I could only guess was an ogre.

"Well, now you've seen them. What do you want to do?" Tennyson asked.

"I'm going to kill them," I said.

"Grace," Troy said to warn me.

"No, Troy, she's right. We are going to kill them as an example," Levi said.

"I should have known you'd lose your senses when you married her," Troy teased.

"He hasn't had any for a while," Tennyson added. I nudged him with my shoulder, and he chuckled.

"I say we let them inside, and I will ice cube them," I said.

"We want to have fun, too," Levi teased.

"I'll leave a couple for you. I need you to create the illusion that we've stepped out of the protective ward sooner than we actually have, so that we can draw them past the border," I instructed him.

"Sure. Move the border," he smirked.

"If you can't do it, then just say so," I teased.

"I can, but that means I'll be focused on the magic instead of getting to kill things," he said gripping, Excalibur by his side. "And I'm going to need the book."

"Go get it," I said.

He blinked out of sight, then quickly back with the book in hand.

"I say we move to the road to do this," Tennyson said, holding his sword. Troy pulled Driggs from the holsters under his suit. He nodded that he was ready.

As I walked out of the forest, I touched the trees pulling power.

"The Queen is welcome to our magic," one said to me. I thanked it silently.

"The time has come for the Queen to rise," the next one said.

When my hand touched the last one, it said, "All hail, Gloriana, Queen of the Exiles and the Winter Realm."

Pride welled up inside of me. The job I'd never wanted was mine, and so many things had changed. I didn't fear the darkness. In fact, I pulled upon it, transforming my wedding dress into a shimmering silver dress with a low-cut front and a very short bottom. I heard Levi growl in approval beside me. The unicorn crown appeared on my head, and I pulled the hilts of my daggers out of my bra. Tennyson snorted, but raised his sword.

"Walk forward in a line. I will walk right behind you to cast the illusion," Levi instructed.

Icy blades extended from the hilts in my hands, as Tennyson, Troy and I approached the fairies on the border. I felt Levi's magic swirl around us as we came into sight.

We stopped slightly short of the real border. The wild fairies sneered at us as the big one approached. He stopped short of the real border. I held my breath hoping that I could provoke them to step inside.

"Leave this place. You are not welcome here," I announced.

The ogre laughed and it echoed through the trees. "We have come to kill you, Gloriana, on behalf of our Queen."

"I am your Queen," I replied.

"You are the Queen of misfits and rejects. The Wild rule Winter now," he said.

"Who leads you?" I asked.

"We lead ourselves," he replied.

"Color me unimpressed," I smirked.

"We follow King Brockton," he added as if it were rehearsed. I felt the lie like a touch of magic, and it held no power over me.

"That is not true. I always knew the Wild were liars without honor," I accused.

"I speak the truth," he growled. His voice rumbled the trees once again.

"You think you can kill me?" I asked, tapping my ice blades together.

His eyes cut to my knives and then back to me with an evil smile. His spiked teeth appeared, and he began to laugh. His olive skin shook as he mocked me. Watching the real border with my sight, I saw as he stepped one foot forward. It barely crossed the border. I couldn't spook him before the others crossed.

"You think you will fight me with those little knives? You can beat this?" He reached behind his head and pulled a hulking poleaxe from his back. The axe blade edge flickered with the light of the rising sun.

"Why don't you come and see?"

The other fairies gathered behind him as he stepped fully behind the ward. I looked back to Levi who held the book, chanting quietly.

"I'll kill the others first, so you can watch," the ogre said as he approached. Almost half of the group had crossed the border.

Troy focused his pistols on the group, as Tennyson settled into a fighting stance. I twirled one of my icy blades around in my hand as if I weren't scared of the ogre. I wasn't so much as I was hoping that his last man would cross the border before I came within reach of that long axe.

I felt the last one cross as I came within swinging distance of the axe. Troy rolled to my left, firing both guns at targets. One exploded into goo while the other howled as his skin ignited into flame. The ogre lunged at me with his axe. I stepped sideways as Tennyson planted his sword in the neck of a troll. He jerked it back, then swiped the entire head off with one swing. The sheer power behind his strike was impressive. The other troll, who wasn't as big as the ogre, but definitely uglier, charged Troy.

"Grace!" Levi exclaimed as I ducked another swinging blow by the ogre.

"You do that. Don't worry about me," I instructed. He grimaced and continued the chant.

Troy fired Driggs multiple times into the troll. The body of the beast shook with the electricity and the fire rippled over his skin, but he continued to charge. Troy shifted and took the blow of the ogre. When the troll rolled over, the wolf had his teeth buried into his neck. Troy jerked a chunk of flesh from its neck, and it fell limp. Troy shifted back, naked as a jaybird, and lifted his pistols again.

We'd had our fun, and I didn't know how long I'd be able to dodge the poleaxe. Pulling on the power of Winter, the sky darkened, and snow began to fall. The horde realized they had been tricked, but it was too late. I dropped my blade and forced Winter out of my hands and into their bodies freezing them solid. Except the ogre, who had turned to run for the border. From his feet up, he began to freeze to the asphalt.

"I am Gloriana, Queen of the Winter Realm and the Exiles, and I told you to leave," I growled, clinching my hands together forming a fist. The minions who were ice cubes, exploded in a mass of ice and dust. Except for one. I had plans for him.

The ogre chopped at the ice on his legs, but as he chipped it off more formed. I stepped in front of him, watching the ice over-take his body. Winter flowed through me, and I felt my eyes flip from turquoise to pure white of snow.

"Shit," Levi muttered.

"*I am under control,*" I told him.

"*I know you are, but you look badass,*" he said with admiration.

The ogre stood in front of me. His eyes twitched but the rest of him couldn't move.

"I warned you," I said, allowing Winter to well up inside of me. With my tiny fist, I slammed it into the ice shattering the ogre into a million icy bits.

"Damn. That was impressive," Troy said.

Releasing the power inside of me, I began to shake my hands. Levi closed the book and rushed to me. He wrapped me up in his arms.

"*That is the last time I sit on the sidelines,*" he complained.

"*We couldn't have done it without the illusion,*" I reminded him.

"*Well, then we are going to have to find another bard,*" he said.

I sighed. "*Then we will have to make one,*" I replied, looking up into his deep blue eyes.

"Make one, make one?" he asked, lifting an eyebrow.

"Yep," I replied.

"Maybe one day," he replied.

"Whatcha going to do with this one?" Tennyson asked, staring at the last block of ice.

"Oh, he's going to be our messenger. Get ready to grab him. I'm going to release him," I said.

Troy and Tennyson positioned themselves on each side of the bogan as the ice began to melt around him. They grabbed him by the arms as soon as he thawed. He fell to his knees in front of me.

"Thank you, my Queen for sparing my life," he whimpered.

"You will go to the Winter Court and tell my Uncle Brockton that I'm coming for him," I said.

"No, please, my Queen. I beg you to allow me to stay here," he said.

I shook my head. "It's too late for that, you had your choice," I replied.

"I won't go back. She scares me. She scares all of us. She's evil incarnate. Please do not send me back," he begged.

"Who is she?" I asked.

"She is the Queen of the Wild," he replied.

"What is her name?" I demanded.

"Onoskelis," he replied. I was shocked. I fully expected him to name Lisette. Onoskelis was a demon woman with a half-mule body. Her true form was said to be made of seven dead witches. I thought back to the demon that Levi had called. Maybe he hadn't called a demon at all. Perhaps Shanaroth was working for Onoskelis, in order to deceive Levi. We already knew they were looking for ways to kill him. I wondered why she hadn't just done it herself.

"A demon," Tennyson said.

"Is she called Lisette?" I asked the bogan.

"By some," he replied.

Levi sank to the pavement, holding the book. I rushed over to him, forcing him to look at me.

"I slept with a demon," he sighed.

"Some have called me a demon," I said.

"But you aren't," he said.

"Technically, neither is she. She's a Wild fairy that needs to be contained or killed. Have you ever heard of Yuki-Onna?" I asked.

"No," he muttered.

"She's a succubus that lures men to her. She freezes them and steals their soul. Sound familiar?" I asked.

"Is that based on you?" he asked.

"Loosely based," I said with a smile. "Levi, you gotta put that behind you. You were deceived, and it was no simple deception. Although, I've heard Onoskelis was fond of butt stuff." His eyes shot to mine. "Oh, so that part is true."

"Grace," he groaned.

"Git your ass off. I mean, get off your ass. If we all took time to lament the times we've fucked a demon, we'd be here all day," I said.

"Hold up. Leave me out of that," Troy said.

"Amanda Capps came here with less than honorable intentions," I said.

He gulped. "That's true."

I looked at Tennyson who shook his head. "And ol' Lance over here has wild hentai sex with his grindy."

Levi snorted. "And what about you?"

"Too many to count," I said.

"Really?" he asked.

"Okay, only one," I replied.

"I'm sorry. I lost sight for a moment," he said.

"We all do from time to time," Tennyson said. "I spent too many years separated from my King."

"You have redeemed yourself," I said.

"Not yet. But I will," he replied.

"We don't have to send him to them. They will know we killed them," Levi said.

"Probably," I said with a snap. The bogan dusted into tiny ice particles. My glamour shifted back to my wedding dress which was disheveled.

"Time to go home?" Levi asked.

"No, I want all of them dead. How many more are out there?" I asked Troy.

"Two other smaller groups. One west of town, the other to the Northeast," he replied.

"Let's dust."

CHAPTER SEVENTEEN

WE RETURNED HOME EXHAUSTED. BOTH GROUPS OF WILD FAIRIES FELL for the ruse, but neither had an ogre leading them which sucked, because I'd enjoyed punching him into icy dust. Winter pulsed through my veins, and I pressed back the darkness. The love of the kill. The thrill of power coursing through my body.

"We will need that power and more when we get to Winter," Tennyson said as if he could read my thoughts.

"I'll be ready," I replied. I had my life preserver, Levi. He could bring me back from anything. I knew he would.

"Get some rest," Tennyson said.

Troy followed him out the door. Callum rose up from the couch where he had been asleep.

"You guys okay?" he asked.

"Yeah, we are fine. Go back to sleep," I said.

Nestor appeared in the kitchen holding two cups of steaming coffee.

"Bless you, Nestor," I said.

Levi and I joined him in the kitchen. We talked in low tones telling him what happened with the wild fairies on the borders, and what we had learned about Lisette.

"What about Frist?" I asked.

"None of your business," Nestor said.

"I know, but I asked anyway."

"No honeymoon?" Nestor asked, changing the subject.

"We had a pre-wedding honeymoon," I replied.

"Whatever! We are still going on a honeymoon," Levi said, finishing off his coffee.

"Levi, we have a house full of people and too much to do," I said.

He took the coffee cup from my hand and gave it to Nestor. "Come," he said, offering his hand to me

"Levi," I protested.

A chord played on his guitar, and I felt my will bend to his. I fought it, but it was too seductive. I shook my head but gave him my hand.

"Keep an eye on the house, Ness," Levi instructed.

"Gotcha," Nestor replied with a smile.

Levi produced Excalibur out of thin air, giving it a half-hearted twirl. A portal opened up next to him. He stepped through pulling me with him.

A green meadow spread out before us filled with a multitude of wild flowers. Bees and butterflies flirted with the blooms. The sky above us was warm, but all of the humidity of Shady Grove was gone.

"Summer," I said.

"Yes, Astor arranged a little getaway for us," Levi said, wrapping his arms around my waist from behind. He gently forced me to turn around. Along the tree line of a forest, a small cabin sat with sweet flower boxes under the windows. A stone path led up to the wooden door with large metal hinges. It looked cozy and inviting.

"Not many Southern brides can claim their honeymoon was in the fairy realm," I said.

"Well, I have connections," Levi said.

"It could have been the trailer and I would have been just as happy," I said to him.

"Trailer, I'm sure, but not a condo or a beach house, I'm willing to bet," he replied. His voice brushed past my ear giving me chills.

"Trailer is better," I responded.

"No need to be concerned. Joey has a unit of centaurs out here guarding the perimeter," Levi explained.

"I'm not concerned," I replied. "I am quite horny though."

"Grace, don't be so vulgar," he said. The romantic in him cringed at my dirty mouth, but it turned him on. I could feel it.

"I'll be vulgar until the day I die," I said as I turned to face him.

"I guess I better get used to it," he said.

"Or you could make me behave," I replied.

His eyes lit up with the implication. "Are you giving me permission?"

I took a deep breath. "Yes."

He spun me around and popped me on the ass. "Get over to that house!" he ordered with a chord on the guitar.

It didn't sink in as much as he wanted, because it was a half-hearted command. I had the feeling he would always give me a choice. "Yes, sir," I replied, rubbing my butt where he slapped me. It didn't hurt, but I was playing along. He marched along behind me chuckling.

When we got to the door, he opened it for me.

"Come in, my Queen," he said, waving to the inside of the tiny cabin.

The fire blazed lazily in the fireplace, but I felt no heat from it. A large, soft bed sat opposite the fireplace. There was a small table with two chairs. On the table, a basket sat with a tag.

Lifting the tag, I read, "To the King and Queen of Winter, welcome to your Summer cabin. It is yours to use whenever you please. Enjoy each other. All our love, Astor and Ella."

We opened the basket to find two bottles of Astor's wine and various chocolates and summer fruits. Levi leaned in over my shoulder. "Hmm. Those look good," he said. His voice rippled over my skin.

"What the hell?" I muttered, looking down at my arm.

"You just *thought* you knew the power of a love talker," Levi said.

"You are not my first love talker, Levi Rearden," I said.

"I guarantee I'm a lot less honorable than the last one," he purred in my ear.

"Holy shit," I cursed. Each word vibrated inside of me. If he kept talking, I might orgasm with just his voice. I felt his hand rub up my back to grab the zipper on my dress. I was practically reeling when he knelt behind me to kiss the base of my back. Pulling the dress to the floor, he exposed the remaining garter along with some very sexy underwear and a white corset that I didn't realize I was wearing. My fairy godmother was very talented.

Levi kissed down my leg to the garter. "You will have to just keep that on, because I've pulled one too many of those off today."

I giggled, but each kiss sent me to the edge of an orgasmic oblivion. Then I felt nothing as he moved away from me. He grabbed one of the chairs and plopped down in it. He slid out of his jacket and pulled his tie loose.

"Come to me," he ordered softly.

My legs obeyed, and I didn't fight it. He smiled up at me and patted his lap. I sat down straddling his legs. He ran his hands up my legs causing me to shudder with anticipation.

"Levi," I rasped.

"Oh, no, my Queen. This will be very slow. There will be no rushing today," he said. "Help me with my shirt."

My urge was to rip it off him, but his power overruled mine. I fumbled with the buttons as he admired me. His eyes wandered over all of my body. He leaned forward as I pulled the shirt out of his pants and pushed it off his arms. It hung on the back of the chair. He shifted his weight below me, and he was just as turned on as I was.

"What now?" I asked.

"Kiss me," he said. I wanted to devour him, but he controlled the long slow kisses. His tongue teased my lips, then he pulled away. "Stand up." I stood up before him, unable to resist his order. "Turn." He pressed his lips on my left cheek, then my right. With a tug, he began to unlace the corset, slowly unthreading each piece of the ribbon that held it together. My body hummed, craving his touch. I'd never felt anything like it.

The corset hit the floor with a thud, and I jumped because I'd become so in tune with his movements and his touch that it startled me. His fingers softly travelled up and down my back, caressing my skin to a crescendo. He knew it too. Every time I reached that tipping point, he backed off.

He stood up behind me without touching me. "Take off my pants," he said.

When I faced him, I wanted to smack the smile off his face, but I couldn't do anything except obey. I pushed his pants and boxers to the floor. He stepped backward out of them, taking my hand. He guided me to the edge of the bed.

"Levi, if you don't hurry up," I whispered.

"I told you. I was taking my time, and so will you," he said. I groaned. "Put your hands on the bed."

"Fuck," I muttered, putting my hands on the bed. I had to bend over slightly. He stood behind me, hooking my teeny lacy panties with his finger. He dragged them down my legs to the floor. Then, he popped me on the ass again.

"That's for your vulgar mouth." He laughed.

"You love my vulgar mouth," I replied.

"I do, and that's why you are about to use it," he replied. I shut my mouth and wished I hadn't goaded him. But part of me loved the thrill of him being in control. He knew what I liked and didn't like. We'd talked about the things that weren't turn-ons for me. I didn't like any hardcore stuff. He assured me that he would never do anything I didn't want. I wanted whatever he'd give me at this point. I sank to my knees and looked up to him.

"I'm ready," I said.

THE FIRE FLICKERED through the rest of the day and the night as Levi and I enjoyed a day of pure passion. He even taught me how to do the bard thing, and I could control him if I wanted. I learned the power of it really manifested in the desire to fulfill your partner completely in a sensual manner. Levi was right. I'd never experienced anything like it before.

"You have been holding back," I accused him while we laid in the bed tangled up in each other.

"Yes," he said quietly.

"Why?" I asked.

"I wanted you to have something special on your wedding night. You've fulfilled all my dreams. It was the least I could do," he said.

"So damn romantic."

"Always."

"It was so good."

"I know."

"Levi Rearden!" I popped him on the arm, and he laughed.

"We have to go back."

"I know."

"Astor gave me the cabin. It's ours. We can come here whenever we want. I imagine there will be times when we just need a break from the craziness of fairies."

"I'll be sure to thank him."

"You can, but your faith in him to be the King of Summer meant everything to him."

"Then we will build a magical cabin for him and Ella in Winter."

"That's a wonderful idea, Grace."

"Yeah, why didn't you think of it?"

"I dunno. Guess I've rubbed off on you."

"And in me."

"And in you." He kissed me on the temple. "Was it too much?"

"What?"

"The control?"

"The control over me?"

"Yeah."

"I fought it, but you only met my needs. Granted you teased me more than I expected."

"But you liked it?" It was definitely a question, not a statement.

"I loved it."

"I can do it again sometime?"

"Absolutely." I don't think I'd ever see him smile so much. I took my pillow and bopped him in the head with it.

"Hey!"

"Aw, poor Levi!'

He tackled me in the bed and began to tickle me. I screamed for him to stop, but he wouldn't. I tried fighting him. He wasn't mentally controlling me. He was just more muscular and physically imposing than he looked. Finally, he relented as I tried to regain my breath. He held my hands on the bed at both sides of my head. Leaning down over my lips, I waited for the kiss. But the tease master, rolled off of me.

"Time to get up!" he said.

"Fucking tease!" I yelled, throwing all the pillows at him.

"You are going to throw one of those in the fire and burn down our cabin!" he warned.

I threw my hand at the fire, forcing Winter power to it, but it didn't go out.

He died laughing, then stuck his hand in the fire.

"It's not a real fire, silly woman."

"Oh. Magic?"

"Yeah. It's for ambiance. It's too hot in Summer to have a real fire."

A light knock at the door interrupted our enjoyment. Levi pulled his pants on and opened the door with Excalibur in his other hand, hidden from the visitor.

"You have to come home," Astor said.

"What's wrong?" I asked, holding the sheet up in front of me.

"Winnie."

CHAPTER EIGHTEEN

REACHING OUT TO FEEL MY CHILD, I RAN THROUGH THE WOODS BEHIND the house to where I could feel her. When we returned to the house, Nestor told us that the wolves, Callum, and Aydan were out looking for her. No one could pick up the scent. Even LeAnne, the Valkyrie, was out looking. I didn't understand how she could have gotten out of the house.

As I ran, a smaller wolf ran past me in the direction where I sensed my child. He reached her before me. His growl rumbled through the forest. Levi ran on my heels with Troy.

"Mark, stand down," he yelled at the pup.

Mark snarled at the boy who stood next to Winnie holding a knife. He dropped the knife and backed away from Winnie.

"You always ruin everything," Winnie yelled at Mark. He stopped barking, but still watched the boy. I recognized the kid as Kyrie, Niles Babineau's son.

"I'm sorry," the boy said.

"What is going on here?" I demanded of the children.

Levi reached down and picked up the knife. "This belongs to Callum. It's a family heirloom," Levi said.

"Winnie, did you steal Callum's knife?" I asked.

"Mark, come here," Troy demanded. The little wolf obeyed his alpha. He trotted behind his father and shifted back to human. Troy took off his t-shirt and put it over Mark's head. The shirt hung down to his knees.

A large white raptor soared between the trees and landed nearby as a white wolf ran up out of the other side of the woods. They shifted as they came closer to us.

Callum panted. "We looked everywhere for you! I couldn't get a scent."

Winnie bit her bottom lip and looked back and forth at us.

"Somebody better start talking," I said.

"I know what she did," Mark said boldly.

"Shut-up, Mark," Winnie whined.

"Wynonna Riggs, start talking," I said.

Levi knelt down in front of her. She started shaking her head as he looked at her. "Winnie, you've scared all of us. Tell us what's going on," Levi coaxed.

I swallowed my fear which was coming off as anger and took Levi's cue. "We love you, baby. Why are you out here in the woods with Kyrie?"

"She said she would give me the knife," Kyrie said.

Tears silently slipped down Winnie's cheeks. "I need to know," she said.

"Know what?" Levi asked.

"I need to know what it feels like to rise," she said.

I gasped and turned my face from her. It was like I had been stabbed in the heart. Levi wrapped an arm around me.

"Princess, you are too young to worry about that," Levi said. "You gotta learn to control all your other powers."

"But if I can rise, then Aydan won't have to take my place," she said.

"Take your place?" Levi asked.

"She means back when I took her place with the witch," Aydan said.

"If I can rise, then Aydan won't get killed. I can do it," she said. In the simplest way, she wanted to protect her brothers as they had protected her. I couldn't fault her for being just like her daddy.

"How did you get out of the house?" Aydan said, kneeling next to her.

"Like this," she said.

"I'll be damned," Troy muttered.

"Grace, look," Levi coaxed me.

I turned to see an exact copy of Callum. The original looked mortified. Switching to my sight, I saw my daughter under the glamour.

"Where did you learn to do that?" I asked softly.

"I dunno. I just tried it one day and it worked. It's like when you aren't the ice queen," she said shyly. Winnie had more gifts that needed developing. We had been so consumed with fighting for the exiles and getting married that some of her training had gone to the wayside.

"I'm sorry, Winnie," I said.

"No, I'm sorry, Momma," she said.

"We have been very busy with the bad guys and getting married. We love you very, very much, and we want to help you learn to do all these things. Most importantly, you've got to learn when to do them, and when not to do them," I said.

"I'm sorry, Mark," she said to the little wolf.

"Don't ever ask me to do that again," he snorted.

She hung her head.

"She asked you to stab her?" Troy asked.

"She did. Then, she got mad at me because I refused," Mark said.

"Son, that is something you should have told us."

"I thought since I told her no that she would give it up."

"Looks like you need to learn a lesson, too," Troy said. "I'm sorry, Grace. I had no idea."

"It's okay. They are learning. It's not like human kids. They face things that most kids don't," I said.

"I'll take Kyrie home and talk to Niles," Troy said. Kyrie joined Mark as they followed Troy back to the house.

"Can we go back home?" Winnie asked.

"Sure," Levi said, helping me up. He picked up Winnie who was getting too big to pick up. She wrapped her arms around his neck and cried the whole way home.

* * *

AFTER AN EXHAUSTING TALK WITH WINNIE, we'd learned that she knew a lot more than she let on around us. Especially about her fairy powers. I had always feared the phoenix stuff because I didn't understand it. But the devil I knew scared me more. I knew what I was capable of, and I hoped that we could keep her on the right track. She'd been through so much in her short little life. Never knowing her biological father. Her mother's death. Dylan's death. All the crazy fairy stuff. Levi and I getting married. It was a lot for a little girl to handle. Levi and I promised to do better.

Nestor consoled us. "Most parents want to do the best by their children, but sometimes they have to make sacrifices. Winnie is a good girl. We will all do better to understand what is going on in that little head. You can't beat yourself up about it."

Winnie had admitted that her version of Mark not playing with her was that he wouldn't help her die so she could rise. I just wished he had told us. She still was curious, and I knew one day she might have to experience it. I just hoped that she would gain some perspective about it before her curiosity won out. I knew how powerful Dylan was and how much he refused to use that power. With Winnie, she didn't have the years of discipline that Dylan had had.

We decided to have a family day. We kept everyone else out of the house. Astor had taken Ella and their twins home. He told us that they named them Rory and Ruby. Fitting names considering their ginger heritage.

I cooked spaghetti. The boys played Monopoly with Winnie, and

Nestor mingled back and forth between the kitchen and the living room. I finally got bold enough to ask again about Kathrine Frist.

He laughed. "You aren't going to give it up, are you?"

"She is well-known to have multiple dead husbands."

"For the record, I'm not the marrying type. Secondly, those are rumors. Katie has the same problems as the rest of us. We are always made out to be the bad guy."

"You have to admit she isn't the nicest person."

"She's nice to me."

"You are dicking her."

"Grace!" Levi interjected.

"Sorry," I mumbled.

"Damn, Levi. You got her straight already," Nestor teased.

"I wish," he replied.

"He does not wish. He likes me wild and stubborn," I said.

"Maybe a little," Levi admitted. "Go play with the kids. I can finish these dishes." I kissed him on the cheek, then went to see who I could help with the game. Winnie was beating both of the boys, so I decided to stay out of it.

When Aydan ran out of money, she jumped for joy. "I won! I won! I won!"

Aydan looked disgusted, but Callum gave her a high-five.

"I'm pretty sure she cheated," Aydan groaned.

"You gotta watch her. She's a smart girl," I said. She hugged me.

"I beat the boys!"

"You did. Great job. I'm so proud," I replied.

She did a little victory dance while Aydan put up the game. I coaxed my daughter off cloud nine. Just as we put her to bed, Dominick arrived at the house. He sat down with Levi and I. Nestor had already gone home.

"Did you find anything?" I asked.

"I guess you know it's Lisette, now," he replied.

"Yes, and that she is considered a demon by some. Very powerful."

"Yes. She is definitely Lysander's grand-daughter, which makes her your half-sister. She's as much your blood as Finley. Has he returned?" Nick asked.

"Not yet," I replied.

"Folks down there remember Lysander visiting her and a woman who was her mother. He apparently made an impression on quite a few women down there. Some of them were disappointed that he was dead. They would have liked to have done it. He's got at least three illegitimate kids down there."

"Are they fairy? Like who leads them?" I asked.

"I couldn't get much out of them, but they were organized and protected," he said.

"Maybe it's your mother," Levi suggested.

"Maybe, but I don't see Mom living in a little bayou town like that," I said.

"It's tiny. Like 3 square miles," Nick said.

"Go get some rest. Thank you for going down there. Did you see any of the packs while you were there?" I asked.

"Yes, and none of them were friendly. I met up with a loner friend of mine. I brought him back with me, if that is okay," Nick said.

"Of course. I look forward to meeting him," I said.

"Thank you, Grace."

"Go sleep, Brother," Levi said, clasping hands with Dominick.

Levi and I went to bed but spent most of the night talking about possibilities to take Lisette out. We figured she was the real power down there considering her ties to my father. As far as I was concerned, she wasn't any kin of mine. I wondered how many other children my father had rejected. Who else would come for me because he scorned them? It didn't matter. One crisis at a time. No sense in making it worse.

Bramble and Briar had been quiet since the death of their friend. They still followed Winnie around for the most part but apologized for not being with her when she coaxed Kyrie into trying to kill her. They had been attending Thistle's funeral pyre.

Winnie had promised to give Kyrie Callum's knife. Kyrie had Native American ties, and he wanted the knife for those reasons.

We waited through the next day, and Finley did not come home. Riley was distraught. I hated that we had sent him back in there. But when he showed up two days later, I was thankful that we had.

After he reunited with his wife, he joined us along with the other knights at the trailer office.

"It is Lisette, which I guess you know. The Wild consider her their Queen, but not all of them are there with Winter to fight against us. Everyone in the castle fears her. She did marry Brockton, but it made him more legitimate to your father's crown," Finley said.

"She married her uncle," I scowled.

"Thin blood connection there," Levi said.

"Still, Winter ain't Alabama," I scoffed.

"What about the forces?" Tennyson asked.

"The Wild control the castle. The harpies have not returned to serve the new King and Queen," Finley said. "But I'd say their force is a hundred thousand strong."

Astor whistled, and Levi groaned.

"I just need to sit on my father's throne. We don't have to kill them all. I just have to show them who is in control," I said.

"You will have to kill her to get on it. She sits her pretty butt there most of the day. She knows the moment she gives it up that she will lose it. She knows we are coming," Finley said.

"Good. Because when I get there, I'm going to rip her eyes out of her head."

"Too bad Jeremiah didn't finish the job when he went after her," Troy said.

"Can't blame him. I had her here too, but I let her go," I said. "I was naïve to think she would go back to the swamps and be a good little witch."

"When do we move out?" Luther asked.

"Tomorrow," Tennyson said.

"Good. Because I'm about to pitch the biggest hissy fit known to the whole world and the one below," I said.

149

Pitchin' a Hissy Fit will be released in late June/early July. Check my website and facebook group for updates.

* * *

Please consider leaving a review for Fit to Be Tied if you enjoyed the book. As an independent author, positive reviews go a long way to helping me get more visibility for my work.

CROÍROINNTE

CAST OF CHARACTERS

Grace Ann Bryant- Exiled fairy queen hiding in Shady Grove, Alabama. Daughter of Oberon. Also known as Gloriana, to her Father and the fairies of the Otherworld. She was called Hannah while traveling with the gypsy fairies before coming to North America. Owns a dachshund named Rufus. Loves orange soda and Crown. Nickname: Glory

Dylan Riggs- Sheriff of Loudon County, Alabama. Fiancé to Grace Ann Bryant. The last living Thunderbird and the only living Phoenix. Also known as Serafino Taranis and Keme Rowtag. Died saving his daughter, Winnie. Nickname: Darlin'

Levi Rearden- Changeling from Texas brought to live with Grace by Jeremiah Freyman. Given Bard powers by Oberon. Looks good in a towel. Engaged to Grace after he rescues her from the Summer Queen, Rhiannon. Nickname: Dublin

Wynonna Riggs- formerly known as Wynonna Jones, but adopted by Grace and Dylan. Human daughter of Bethany Jones who dies in

Tinsel in a Tangle. Given the power of the Phoenix by her father. Nickname: Winnie, Wildfire

Aydan Thaddeus Riggs- son of Dylan Riggs and Grace Ann Bryant. Heir to Thunderbird inheritance. Rapid aging caused Aydan to seem like he's 18 years old.

Callum Fannon- Cherokee white wolf shifter. Lives with Grace and family. Calls Grace, Mom. Approx. 20 years old.

Nestor Gwinn- Grace's maternal grandfather. Kelpie. Owner of Hot Tin Roof Bar in Shady Grove. Maker of magical coffee.

Troy Maynard- Police chief in Shady Grove. Wolf shifter. Married to **Amanda Capps** and father to his adopted son, **Mark Capps (Maynard)** who is Winnie's best friend. New father to three girls.

Betty Stallworth- wife to Luther Harris. Waitress at the diner. Flirts with everyone. Banshee.

Luther Harris- head cook at the diner. Makes good gravy biscuits. Ifrit.

Tabitha Mistborne- fairy physician. Daughter of Rhiannon. Dated Remington Blake. Died after betraying Grace and the Exiles.

Mable Sanders- former spy for Oberon. Fairy Witch. Girlfriend of Nestor Gwinn. Member of the ORCs. Once known as Mab, the Winter Queen.

Sergio Krykos- Grace's Uncle who has taken over the Otherworld. In his first life, he was known as Mordred, half-brother to King Arthur. Goes by the name Brockton.

Oberon- King of the Winter Otherworld. Grace's father. In his first life, he was known as King Arthur.

Rhiannon- Queen of the Summer Otherworld. Half-sister to Oberon. In her first life she was known as Morgana, a fairy witch. Killed by Levi.

Robin Rayburn- daughter of Rowan. Embodiment of Titania, the former Summer Queen. Member of the ORCs. Killed by Grace after she threatened Aydan.

Cohen- mentioned as a former king after Arthur. Grace's first human world lover. Exiled and forsaken.

Remington Blake- Grace's ex-boyfriend. Dating Tabitha Mistborne. From N'awlins. Sweet talker. One of the Native American Star-folk.

Astor Knight- The ginger knight that Grace brought back from the Summer realm. Formerly betrothed to Grace. Former First Knight of the Tree of Life. In his first life, he was Percival, Knight of the Round Table. Married to Ella Jenkins.

Soraya Harris- Jinn granddaughter of Luther Harris. Living in Shady Grove. Has connections to the world in-between life and the afterlife.

Matthew Rayburn- Druid. Spiritual leader of Shady Grove. Leads services in a Baptist Church which is a portal into the Summer Realm. Enthralled by Robin Rayburn.

Kadence Rayburn- Daughter of Matthew. Ex-girlfriend of Levi. Enthralled by Malcom Taggert. Becomes a fairy. Dating Caleb Joiner.

Malcolm Taggart- Incubus that once tried to seduce Grace. Enthralls Kady. Executed by Grace.

Caleb Joiner- Lives with Malcom and Kady, but frees Kady from Malcolm.

Riley McKenzie- Daughter of Rhiannon and Jeremiah Freyman. Levi's ex-girlfriend. Stole the songbook. Fled the Summer Realm with Grace. Marries Finley becoming Riley Bryant, Grace's sister-in-law.

Stephanie Davis- Daughter of Rhiannon. Dylan's ex-girlfriend. Sergio Krykos' ex-girlfriend. Mother to Devin Blankenship. Missing in the Winter Otherworld. Killed by Levi. Reincarnated with no memories of past deeds.

Joey Blankenship- Tryst with Grace. Enthralled by Stephanie. Father to Devin Blankenship. Turned into a faun by Rhiannon. Escapes the Summer Realm with Grace and his son. Now the head of the army in Summer under King Astor.

Eugene Walter Jenkins- Mayor of Shady Grove. Former Knight of the Round Table, Ewain. Wife died in childbirth. Father to Ella Jenkins. Partner to Charles "Chaz" Leopold.

Eleanor "Ella" Jenkins- Changeling daughter of Mayor Jenkins. Teacher at the fairy school. Marries Astor. Pregnant with twins.

Charles "Chaz" Leopold- Also known as "The Lion." Hairdresser. Second Queen in Shady Grove.

Finley Bryant- Grace's "twin" brother. Wears armor portraying the symbol of Grace's royalty. Marries Riley McKenzie.

Jenny Greenteeth- A grindylow living in Shady Grove. In her first life, she was known as Guinevere, wife of Arthur, lover of Lancelot. Cursed to her current form.

Tennyson Schuyler- Mob boss. In his first life, he was known as Lancelot, Knight of the Round Table. Oberon calls him Lachlan.

Cletus and Tater Sawyer- Last human residents of Shady Grove. Comical, but full of heart.

Yule Lads- A group of Christmas Trolls who moved into town. Lamar is the most frequently mentioned with his various peg legs. Others include: Phil, Cory, Willie, Chad, Keith, Kevin, Phillip, Ryan, Bo, Richard, and Taylor.

Michean Artair- Solomonar. Owner of Magic Vape. Produces magical liquids for all occasions.

Brittany Arizona- Shady Grove's tattoo artist.

Bramble and Briar- Brownies who live in Grace's house, but are attached to Winnie. Hired by Caiaphas to watch over Grace. Now in servitude to Grace.

Caiaphas- Leader of the now defunct Sanhedrin. Formerly known as the wizard, Merlin, but has lost most of his power.

Fordele and Wendy- King and Queen of the Wandering Gypsy Fairies. Fordele was Grace's lover ages ago.

Josey- Grace's former neighbor in the trailer park. Perpetually pregnant. Goddess of the Tree of Life. Also known as Lillith.

Jeremiah Freyman- Deceased. Former member of the Sanhedrin that brought Grace, Dylan, Levi, and most of the other fairies to Shady Grove. Worked for Oberon. Father of Riley. Former Knight of the Round Table. Known as Tristan.

Deacon Giles- Farmer in Shady Grove. Krampus.

Connelly Reyes- First Knight of the Fountain of Youth. Former Knight of the Round Table known as the Grail Knight, Galahad. Best friends with Astor.

Chris Purcell- Winged-werehog. Known as a dealer of information. Settled in Shady Grove with his domesticated wife, **Henrietta.**

Lissette Delphin- Creole Priestess. Tricked Levi into summoning the demon, Shanaroth. One of the ORCS.

Rowan Flanagan- Partner of Tennyson Schuyler. Died in Summer Realm. Mother of Robin Rayburn. In her first life, she was known as Elaine. Mother of Galahad. Took the name Phoebe to marry Remington Blake.

Artemis- Wolf doctor for Troy's pack

Kyffin Merrik- Former partner in Sergio Krykos law firm. Missing.

Demetris Lysander- Grace's former lawyer. Deceased. Aswang.

Phillip Chastain- Judge at Grace's hearing in BYH. Helps with legal matters. Liaison to Human Politicians.

Misaki- Oni disguised as a Kitsune.

Elizabeth Shanteel and Colby Martin- human children murdered in BYH by Demetris Lysander.

Rev. Ezekiel Stanton- Pastor of Shady Grove Church of God. Evacuated when the humans left Shady Grove.

Sylvestor Handley- Michael Handley's father. Blacksmith.

Diego Santiago- Bear shapeshifter. Executed by Grace.

Juanita Santiago- Bear shapeshifter. Widow. Mother of two. Oversees a farm with Deacon Giles help.

Niles Babineau- Developer from New Orleans that helped Remington Blake build more housing in Shady Grove. Returned to New Orleans. Has two children, Celestina and Kyrie.

Jessica- Summer fairy working at the sheriff's office.

Stone and Bronx- Tennyson Schuyler's bodyguards.

Eogan- Treekin in Summer Realm.

Marshall- Captain of the Centaurs in Summer Realm.

Nimue- Lady of the Lake. Keeper of Excalibur. Controls the Water Element Stone.

Brad and Tonya- Brad owns the BBQ joint in Shady Grove. Tonya works there as a waitress.

Katherine Frist- Fairy woman living in Shady Grove known for her many dead husbands. Known as the Black Widow.

Ellessa- Grace's Siren mother. Whereabouts unknown.

Melissa Marx- Levi fangirl.

Taleisin- Bard for Arthur and many other Kings and Rulers. Wrote the songbook given to Levi.

Thistle- Purple haired pixie with a love envelope.

Sandy- Matthew Rayburn's Nurse

Zahir- former knight of the Round Table, Palamedes. Exiled and forsaken for choosing Lancelot's side. Jinn.

Madam Luella Specter- Griffin breeder, also known as Lulu

Tashi- yeti brewmaster

Catrina Moreno- human assassin with a magical tattoo.

LeAnne- Valkyrie brought in to protect the children of Shady Grove, specifically Grace's children.

ACKNOWLEDGMENTS

This book was a struggle to write. I'm not sure why. The first eight chapters were easy-peasy, then once I got past the wedding, it flew out of my fingers. I'm very happy with the end result, and I'm excited for the final two installments of Grace's story.

I want to thank my parents who have helped me out so much with my daughter while my husband and I worked. They have been very supportive of my writing career. I have wonderful parents.

I also have wonderful in-laws. I'm very blessed with two sets of parents who love and care about me and my family.

Thanks to the citizens of the trailer park known as Kimbra Swain's Magic and Mason Jars. You guys are the best. My ARC and BETA teams are fantastic, too!

I also want to thank those citizens who recently joined my Patreon site for a few extras and insights to my work and progress: Liza Marie, Leslie Watts, Faye Bonds, Denise Esh, Bobbie Lawton and Kat HM.

Finally, I want to thank my professional crew, Hampton and Carol. Thank you for all your hard work.

I love you, Jeff and Maleia.

ABOUT THE AUTHOR

From early in life Kimbra Swain was indoctrinated in the ways of geekdom. Raised on Star Wars, Tolkien, Superheroes and Voltron, she found herself immersed in a world of imagination. She started writing in high school, and completed her English degree from the University of Alabama in 2003.

Her writing is influenced by a gamut of authors including Jane Austen, J.R.R. Tolkien, L.M. Montgomery, Timothy Zahn, Kathy Reichs, Kevin Hearne, and Jim Butcher.

Born and raised in Alabama, Kimbra still lives there with her husband and 5-year-old daughter. When she isn't reading or writing, she plays PC games, makes jewelry, and builds cars.

* * *

Join my reader group for all the latest updates on releases, fabulous giveaways, and launch parties.

You can view my publishing schedule on my website.

Follow Kimbra on Facebook, Twitter,
Instagram, Pinterest, and GoodReads.
www.kimbraswain.com

Made in the USA
Middletown, DE
11 October 2020